Broken

Melody Dean Dimick

Coastal Cloud Watcher Press
Beverly Hills, Florida

Book and cover design by Sagaponack Books & Design

www.CoastalCloudWatcher.com

ISBNs:
979-8-9870189-0-3 (softcover)
979-8-9870189-1-0 (hardcover)
979-8-9870189-2-7 (e-book)

Summary: Trapped in a Florida town, plagued by bullies, and intrigued by the other loner, Riley, seeks acceptance and fairytale love, but fears she won't be able to escape the literal and figurative borders built by her survivalist father.

YAF 044000 Young Adult Fiction / Novels in Verse
YAF 011000 Young Adult Fiction / Coming of Age
YAF 037000 Young Adult Fiction / Loners & Outcasts

Coastal Cloud Watcher Press
Beverly Hills, Florida

First Edition
Printed and bound in the USA

Dedicated to the memory of my parents,
Albert and Gertrude Dean …
forever in my heart.

Sometimes the world breaks us.
Imperfections give us beauty.
—the author

FOREWORD

Sadly, one of the first things to come back, after Covid, was gun violence. And it seems to have come back with a vengeance. Yet strangely, it is often avoided in children's literature, or if dealt with, it is from the point of view of victims in need of healing. The perpetrator is a shadowy "other" figure we don't want to know or understand.

That's why to me, *Broken* is ground breaking. It is not only a powerful, lyrical verse novel about a girl named Riley, and her father, a victim of PTSD, who provides the first layer of her understanding. It is also about this same girl accidentally choosing for her first crush, the boy who will turn into a school shooter.

Riley is not a victim in this story, because she refuses to be one. She is also someone who has been close to a perpetrator, and she defends her mixed feelings even in the face of a police investigation. She knows what most of us are afraid to admit—that violent people are not monsters from other dimensions. They are us—if we are broken.

The imagery in the novel is haunting. The compound where Riley's father has sequestered her, surrounded by a jail-like chain-link fence, the lonely swing in the back yard where she watches clouds and dreams of love. The torture on the school bus. And orchids.

And at the center of it all, Dante. The boy Riley struggled to communicate with because she cared about him. The boy who felt the same about her, but only expressed himself in poems she saw after he was dead. This is an important book in the canon or our violent society trying to understand itself. Kids today are going to school in fear. They need books like this one, to help them understand themselves and each other, so this horrible pattern can finally be…broken.

—Joyce Sweeney, literary agent and author

Broken

GRADUATION APPROACHES

I peel an orange,
pour a bowl of cereal,
and glance around the room.
Where's Mom?

I find a note on the kitchen table.
When I read it, my hands tremble
and my hunger disappears—
normally that would be good.

But nothing's normal in my life.
To put it mildly, I'm on edge
when I grab another bowl,
put a spoon and a box of bran

near Dad's spot at the table,
and stuff Mom's instructions
into my bulging backpack.

What surprise?
Mom said she's bringing one.

Will Dad be okay alone all day?
I head to the bus stop,
shivering in the Florida heat.

AIRSTREAM

The school bus hisses and stops.
After locking the chain-link fence
behind me, I grab the handrail and climb
the steep bus steps, but leaving
our tin-can home behind—impossible.

Down the narrow aisle,
trying to squeeze into any spot,
I hear "Keep Out"
from a bigmouth begging for a laugh,
and the snicker of another.

Elbows poke my ribs.
Not in the mood for this.
I swallow anger, refuse to cry,
and mumble, "Deep breaths" ...
Mom's technique to help me cope.

SHAMED

I cringe,
face warm and ketchup-red,
and sneak a glance back
at our shiny silver home swallowed
by Dad's steel fence.

Leaving it behind—my dream—
the impossible dream?
This isn't *Camelot*.

The renovated Airstream
was designed for travel
and adventure. I've read the words *travel*
and *adventure* on the brochure abandoned
on top of the TV cabinet over and over,
anticipating, wanting,
not wanting ...

ABBY

Like a butterfly knife,
Abby's words, "Nobody likes you,"
slice fresh wounds.

I lower my head
as I look for my seat.
The yellow bus lurches.

This seat's saved,
Abby's glare warns.
Her backpack *whumps* onto the seat.

I want to say it's not my fault
two words drip in blood-red
paint across our shiny aluminum
home, shouting, KEEP OUT.

I hate the glistening abomination:
Don't bother us. We're armed.
Dad's Airstream annoys, insults,
forbids, and—
                isolates
                        me.

INTERLOPER

I'm the outsider—
daughter of a wounded veteran.
I sit straitjacket stiff, staring
into space, sharing the bench seat

with Dante Pitt, the other loner.
Dressed in his usual black T-shirt
and jeans, Dante studies the back
of Jamal's head. Neither of us

speaks. Noise makes it a moot
point. From what I've seen,
shouting is not in character
for either Dante or me.

Besides, he's wearing earbuds.
Dante glances my way
a couple of times, and I wonder
if he'll ever speak to me.

Is he sizing me up like the rest?
Does he see heavy breasts
and cottage-cheese thighs
when he sneaks a peek my way?

I wait, worried. What if, when he
finally speaks, he says biting words,
ripping my heart into ragged shreds,
ruining any chance of our hitting it off?

SILENT

As he opens his mouth, I drop
my hair to veil my face.
Does Dante see me shrink?

He tightens his lips.
A knot forms in my belly.
Why am I so ... so me?

Dante's man bun says he's a hipster,
not a goth, but for some reason
I'm the only one at Gertrude Albert
High who thinks he's with-it—edgy—
desirable, possibly a genius—hot.

Something new sparks deep—
deep within from I know not
where. My heart skips
a beat, and I want Dante

to talk to me. *Is this what—
No. It couldn't be.*
Not sure why it's important,
or what I want him to say.
What would I say?

Doesn't seem right
to share a seat on a bus,
unaware of what hides
inside Dante's shell.

The bus belches and halts
in front of the school.
I grab my backpack
and escape without
a single word exchanged—

again.

TEAMS

In gym class, Mortification 101,
I stand on the sideline, shifting
my weight from foot to foot,
staring at my cheap canvas sneakers—

wishing they were Converse.

Anxious—
as wanted
by the team captains
as a case of athlete's foot.

Eager—to play volleyball,
my favorite and best sport.
I pray not to be chosen last,

knowing to fifth-generation Floridians,
I'm the new girl—Yankee—
poison oleander—too toxic to touch.

SEEKING SHELTER

Day ends.
Uneventful ride home,
but I'm sweating—
jumping at sounds.

The bus brakes hiss.
One step at a time
my heavy feet trudge

toward our paint-bleeding
eyesore. Yellow sun shines
off the silver travel trailer,

blinding me for
an instant. I'm
seeking shelter
from school crap
and the blistering heat.

I smirk at the irony
of seeking asylum
in the red-stained
monstrosity we call *home*.

When I reach our steps,
the door's locked.
I fumble inside my blouse
for the brass key, hanging

on the chain, and pray.
Please, God, not today.
Give me a break.

I open the door.

Gasp.

NOT THE ENEMY

Dad's in olive-drab fatigues,
pointing his black rifle
straight at my pounding heart.

"It's me, Dad.
Riley," I whisper.

"You're having a flashback."

No quick moves.

Handle this.

Dad's frozen in a time
long ago, in a desert war.
Before I was born—reliving.

"Breathe, Dad.
Deep breaths."
I gulp for a breath of air.

No quick moves.
Locate and plug in one of the maple-
scented candles Mom leaves on stands.

Not recognizing me isn't Dad's problem.
He isn't even here. *I must trigger*
his senses. Bring him to the present.

"I'm not the enemy. I'm Riley.
We're home—safe. Inhale.
Smell Mom's maple candle."

Gently, I lower my backpack
to the floor, step back, raise
both hands, palms facing
my hypervigilant dad.

I WAIT

I wait
for Dad to return
from the battlefield
and recognize me,
so I can make his dinner.

I wait
to be selected for a team.

I wait for Dante
to speak to me, conning

myself into believing I choose
to wait because, for now,
no action is the best way to make
what I want happen.

Dad squints at me
and lowers his weapon.

I wait
to see what he will do.

I wait
like a stunned sparrow
who's flown into a windowpane,
for my heart to stop thumping.

FEAR

Pausing for my world
to come back to normal anxious,
I wonder if Dad is what
he is because of a gene we share
or because of what he saw
in faraway battles.

Will I be like him?
Can I escape the barrier
Dad built,
fencing us in and others out?

I'm not satisfied with evasions
but fear—answers.

Instead of a necklace,
I wear a heavy chain
with a brass key resting
against my too-ample

cleavage. Chains imprison!
Will I ever escape chains?
Was my wounded dad
ever normal?
Am I?

I cannot live penned
in like a caged tiger.
But I wonder.
Can I leave him behind?

DESTINY

Sometimes I wonder if
it's fitting Dad settled
in this state shaped like a gun—

I wait.
I wonder.
I worry.

*Am I destined to be
my father's keeper?*

*Worse yet, is it
in the stars for me
to follow in his path?*

*Is it in the stars
for Dante and me to move
our relationship forward?
Will he ever kiss me?*

My body trembles.
*Is it fear or anticipation?
What's causing my internal
earthquake?*

CRISIS

I tiptoe to my room.
After about ten minutes, I hear
Dad leave. From my window,
I watch him trudge
toward his greenhouse.

Since I assume he plans to tend
his prize orchids, I put on a pair
of yoga pants and a sleeveless shirt
and amble toward the cornfield,

contemplating what a paradox
Dad is. One minute he waves
an AR-15 at our front door.
The next he nurtures flowers.

He'll be late coming to dinner.
I can take my time—
walk to the edge of our property.

What am I supposed to do?
What more can I do to help
Dad? How can I erase

the vision of Dad's gun aimed at me?

Mom, you left a few instructions
out of your note.
Don't let me make Dad worse.

And, God, don't let him mistake me
for the enemy.

I exhale.

Crisis averted—
for now.

THE NOTE

I reread the note
Mom left on the kitchen table,
to see if I missed a clue
for dealing with a Dad flashback.
What triggered his memory?

Riley,

Sorry I had to leave so abruptly. Will be
back way before graduation with a special
surprise. Please be sure you and your dad
eat. The freezer, cupboards, and refrigerator
are stocked, as usual. LOL. Most of the
vegetables in Dad's garden are ripe. Please
make a salad or tomato sandwiches tonight.
Pick some corn on the cob to serve as
your side and blueberries for cereal in the
morning. I programmed the number for my
burner phone into yours. Call if you can't
handle a situation.

Love,

Mom

No help in the cryptic message.
Can I handle another meltdown?
How long will my therapist Mom be gone?
What special surprise?

RESCUE

Nature beckons. I need her fix
to escape the confines of the trailer.
When I see balloon-like puffs drift
overhead, I throw a blanket

on the cut grass, lie on my back,
and watch Earth's ever-changing
crown. Where did the cloud come from?
Where will it go?

I try to remember
when and why I first wanted clouds
to transport me to exotic places—
Am I a fool for romance?
I've never been kissed by a boy.

Does it matter? Reality intrudes.
Fire ants sting me—make my
skin burn. My eye travels
to our lone majestic live oak tree.

This symbol of Southern tranquility
stretches her long, comforting arms.
Her gray beards of mossy fingers
beckon. The oak entices me ...

like Dante.

CONTRAST

Across the road, no hospitality.
Unkempt. Overgrown lawn.
An abandoned Chevy truck sits on blocks,
and our neighbor's muddy, jacked-up
pickup displays a Southern Cross

on a Confederate flag—waving
me off like Dad's KEEP OUT
sign waves off our would-be visitors.

If my English teacher, Mrs. González,
were here, I'd say, "I get it.
I understand juxtaposition."

LIVE OAK HOSPITALITY

Who could resist a live oak welcome?
Mom calls it nature therapy.
I step closer. Long ago two lovers—

M&B—carved a heart with an arrow
running straight through it,
into the oak's bark. *Did the
graffiti hurt the tree?* I worry.

Wish M and B would have tattooed
the image on their own trunks,
but who knows? Could be, like Mom,
their moms forbid body tattoos.

M or B,
or someone else, hung a rope swing
over one of the oak's limbs.
Hadn't noticed it before. Why?
Captivated, I dash to the tree,

sit on the child's seat made
from a plank of wood, and try
to center myself
while I enjoy nature's movie.

WATCHING CLOUDS

Figures dance in the blue sky,
wearing frilly prom dresses I could
never afford. Silhouettes dart
in front of the scorching sun.

Momentary, mesmerizing clouds
with enchanted silver linings linger.
I dream someday a special someone
will reach down and rescue me.

He'll be another dreamer.
We'll ride double on a black horse.
Silhouettes will gallop in front of the sun.
Bareback, we'll clear rainbows.

Head thrown back, searching.
I'm convinced Earth's
a better place riding two abreast.
I wish for my happily ever after.

Is Dante watching the same clouds?
What does he see?
Is he the one? I daydream.

Two silhouettes emerge in front
of the sun and gallop away
on a black-winged steed.
Ghostlike shadows flit in the air,
circling, threatening to invade.

Fluffy floating clouds move on.
Villainous heavy skies,
casting ominous dark shadows
drift in, blackening the day.

REALITY INTRUDES

Crash! A clap of afternoon thunder
snaps me from my musing.
A miffed mockingbird takes flight.
My Cinderella moment ends.

No glass slipper for me.
I remind myself I can't manage
to get a date to the senior banquet

or someone willing to offer
me a smile and a seat on the bus.
No one's going to scoop

me up and carry me
into the cloudy sunset.
Dante barely knows I exist,

and even if he did, he's got
troubles he's never been willing
to share. We both brood.

PUMPKIN MOMENT

Time to stop living
my life with my head
in passing clouds, waiting
for a knight in dark armor.

Time to do something.
What? First, make dinner!
Mom asks so little of me.

Get a move on.

You've got to write
a spoken-word poem for English
I tell myself.
There's no one else to tell.

CRISIS

I run to the cornfield,
gather four ears of corn.
Angry skies invade,
pelting me with dime-size hail.

When I duck into the greenhouse
for shelter, a gust of wind
accompanies me, creating a draft.

Dad's favorite butter-yellow
orchid with the pastel pink
lip tumbles to the ground.

I panic and stoop
to pick up the four-inch pot
with its delicate bloom.

Where's Dad?
Did he go out the back door?
After putting the pot back,

I glance around. A glint
of steel on the greenhouse
floor catches my eye.

What's this?

GREENHOUSE MYSTERY

Trapdoor? My curiosity awakens,
makes me lift the handle
and peek inside the hatch.
Raisin black shadows. Stairs.

Where do they lead?

Before I take one step,
Dad calls to me.
"Riley, where are you?
Thought I saw you—"

Get out of here.
I let go of the handle,
the bulkhead slams shut—clunk.

Did Dad hear?

I grab the corn. "Coming.
I took cover in the greenhouse
when the rain started."

I raise the bundle of corn.
"I planned to husk
these near the compost pile—"

"I'll do it," Dad says.
"I just repotted an orchid.
Had to wash my hands."

I hand him the corn. He says,
"Go inside and put a kettle
of water on the stove to boil."

From somewhere in my brain,
an unconscious thought escapes:
Dad's a pot ready to boil over—always.

UNMOVING WHEELS

Deep in thought,
I head toward our trailer.
Four wheels to move us,
but we're going no place.

Our wheels haven't moved since
Dad drove fifteen hundred miles
day and night from the shores
of Lake Champlain in New York's
Adirondack Mountain range to this refuge,

escaping from God-knows-what.
Demons? Dogs of war?

In a state flat as a tortilla,
to see the road from my room
I'm forced to look up,
but there are no mountains.

My wannabe-wanderer head
is plagued with the stuck-song
syndrome of Miranda Lambert's
"Airstream Song." Our music teacher

played it for us to teach us to identify chords.
I related to the homemade curtains,
and yearned to be a gypsy,
but like an earworm, my family's burrowed
in. No fun road trip for us after graduation.

POINTLESS!

We have a pointless
KEEP OUT sign.
Our only visitor, Ophelia,
a stray cat I feed on the sly,
prefers to roam outside. I know

her wish, but I scoop her up
and carry her inside.

Wrong, like trapping bees
or butterflies in a mayonnaise jar.

Why do I act so needy?
Am I jealous because she roams free?

KITCHEN SURPRISE

Back in the kitchen,
I root through cupboards.
Pans clang.

A minute later, I'm smiling.

Inside the pot we use to boil corn,
Mom's left a surprise note,
bearing her mantra, a Christopher Robin

quote. "You are braver than you believe.
Stronger than you seem,
and smarter than you think."

She's drawn a little Winnie the Pooh
on the note and printed her familiar
xoxo.

Oh, Mom, hope you're right.

I straighten my back.
Affirm, avow, assert.

Yes, Mom, I can be strong.
I will be strong.
I won't let you down.

FAMILY SECRETS

My troubled mind races.
Dad's storing secrets,
but so am I. We share DNA.
BUT I don't want to become …

Stop! To escape boredom, I raided, digested,
and hoarded the box of romance and poetry
paperbacks Mom bought at a flea market.
Who could discard such gems?

In secret, I practice writing stanzas
with surprise twists. Pour bitterness
like vinegar onto lined pages.
Aim for gut-wrenching truths.

No one knows the lines I've written.
No one knows what will trigger
Dad's next meltdown.
No one knows what I fear.
I keep it hidden.

No one knows what I want.
But Miss Mossy, the librarian, knows I write poems.
Since I'm one of her privileged "Media Rats,"
she lets me listen to our poet laureate
reading poetry on YouTube.

INSPIRED

I'm awestruck.
Joy Harjo's verses inspire me.
Her words strike like lightning bolts.
I want to be a poet.

Oh! Poetry, let me release pent-up frustrations.
Oh! Poetry, let me wage inner war.
Oh! Poetry, let me take Emily Dickinson's
head off her shoulders with icing imagery

or give her a "zero at the bone" moment—
the one I get when I face
down the barrel of Dad's
rifle pointed at my heart

or Zack heading my way in the hall.
I'd settle for writing uplifting
greeting card poetry, easing other's pain.

BLUES

When words fail, I need blues
to express the sorrow of my soul.

No words echo as sad
as my dad's grandfather's harmonica.
No one but Ophelia sees the hand-me-down-
Vietnam Hohner harmonica he gave me.

This obsession rests hidden beneath
my poems. That secret would really
isolate me from classmates and further
                                        set
                                    me
                                        apart.

My harmonica rejuvenates and inspires
me, but to the world, screams uncool loner.

When Great Grandfather showed me how to play,
he started with "The Story of a Soldier,"
and ended with his "Mekong Delta Blues."
"Some call the harmonica a mouth organ,"

he said when he handed it to me.
"I call it a blues harp. Whatever you call it,
no other instrument knows the melancholy
of war like it does."

HE'S RIGHT

Nothing sounds as sad as a harmonica,
except the lullaby of Mom coaxing Dad
back from wherever flashbacks take him.

No one experiences the sadness of war
like silent survivors, but at times when I'm blue
the harmonica and I become one.

Was I born with Dad's blues inside me?

I need to know why his grandfather
went through the Vietnam War
and came back intact, but a war

in a desert traumatized Dad. What did
Dad see? What did he do?
What is he hiding?
Does Mom know?

It doesn't matter.
Answers might make me more of a weirdo.

I write blues poems and songs,
but dare not share family secrets in class.
For those of us broken beyond repair,

safety lies in reciting nonsense rhymes.
Though my isolation shouts and beats
within, it's too private a weight to share.

GLINT OF STEEL

The glint of steel the greenhouse
revealed tells me I'm not the only one
guarding secrets. Dad's got a secret
hidden under the orchids,

and I want to know what
                              it
                                    is.

How can I uncover what's underground
without triggering a Dad meltdown?
What hides beneath the fragile orchids?
What dark memories lie inside Dad?

The need to find out nags me day
and night, but I have to go to school
and leave solving of the mystery for later.

BACKPACK

Usual reaching a seat ordeal.
Abby's snarky remark stings.
"Keep walking, prepper.

Back off. Don't brush
your bug-out bag against me."
Abby fakes fear of my bag.

My backpack isn't a survival bag.
Dad isn't an Oath Keeper,
but I don't respond to her.
I don't own the words to justify
Dad or his warning sign.

As usual, I sit next to Dante.
When the bus gets to the spot
where cell coverage begins,
kids pull out smartphones.

I don't have one.

Dad says phones
let Big Brother breathe
down your neck,
tracing every move you make.

Popular kids sit near friends
on the bus and text each other.

And I'm the strange one?

SAFEGUARD

Without telling Dad,
Mom bought me
one of those burner
phones villains use
on TV crime shows.

It's hidden in my backpack
to be used in an emergency.

We have many crises
at our house, but I've
never called 911.

We keep to ourselves.
Dad fears
              Armageddon.

ALMOST

I glance at Dante.
He's watching me.
He heard the Abby insult.
Our eyes lock.

For a moment, we stare
into each other's eyes—
mesmerized—alone
on a crowded bus. He

inches closer, ever so slowly
closer. My heart races—
anticipating. *It's really going
to happen.* Dante brushes my hair

from my face and whispers,
"I've never had the courage—"

SMACK

A sock ball hits
my cheek, snaps my head
back and rolls to my feet.
My face stings. Tears well.

Martin elbows his way
from three rows back
to our bench seat.
He retrieves his socks.

No words exchanged.
Dante faces the window.
Lip-to-lip contact aborted.

Kiss killed.

JOCKS

Should I have let Mom homeschool me?
I wanted to escape Dad's fence,
but school is a minefield.

Without comment, Coach removes
a noose looped from a gym rafter.
What racist strung it? My body shudders.

Some football-loving classmates terrorize
guys like Dante in the corridors.
Most kids consider sports heroes cool.
Not me. Based on encounters with Zack

and his wingmen, I see our jocks as rude,
sexist—pampered—school society pets.
It shouldn't be this way.
Coach needs to teach them right from wrong.

But he worries about wins, not sportsmanship.

I overheard Zack tell Martin,
"Girls are so clingy. They stick
to you like bloodsuckers."

In the hall when Zack sees Abby,
he hollers, "Hey, Abby, Ma's out of town.
Wanna come over tonight and—"

The rest of his question disgusts me.
What a woman hater.

Unlike Olympic athletes on Wheaties
boxes, Zack doesn't personify what it takes
to be a champion. Far from it.

Abby wants to be popular, so she giggles.
She can have the jocks. Better to be without
a date than to endure constant insults.

Would I cave if offered a date?
No!

CLASS WRITING

Red-penciled
Eliminated
Revised
That's how I feel when I write.
Banned
Refused
Omitted
That's how I feel when I try to connect.
Unwelcome
Different
Bullied
That's how I feel when I look for a bestie.
Fat
Ignored
Withdrawn
That's how I feel in class.
Edgy
Lonely
Dull
I tear up my poem.
And hand in a mundane quatrain.

GYM VICTORY

Despite being picked last, I smile
inside on the way to lunch
because I stuffed Abby, served
three aces, earned four assists,
and spiked the ball for two perfect

kills—
inner victory earned
on a squeaky gym court.

I revealed
my competitive spirit—
so uncharacteristic—
but necessary for survival—

*Oh my God, don't say
the word "survival" out loud.*

KAROL'S OFFER

Karol's cool, not cruel,
but she's afraid of Abby—
the Zack of girls.

When no one's looking,
and Karol and I are alone near
our lockers, she hands me a note:

Sorry, Riley, I know you can play
volleyball, but Abby scares me.
She'd spread crap about me if I chose
you for my team. Call my cell sometime:
352-407-1153. We'll chat.

I could tell you how to dress
in cooler clothes, if you want.
Might help you fit in.
Don't take it the wrong way.
I like how you stand up to Zack.
He trashed me.

    Hugs,
     Karol

I look up to respond, but she's gone.

UNCOMMON

I've never taken a selfie.
I've never posted a TikTok video.
I don't have a learner's permit.
I've never kissed a boy.

A friend to ask for advice
would be nice, but it's always
the same. Most other girls and I
share no common experiences.

Besides, none dare defy Abby's glare.
Abby's just plain rude.
Karol wants to help.
Sees wearing clothes with logos
as the key to acceptance,

but Mom would never allow
me to be a walking ad for any
company. "We don't wear brand names.
You have your own name," she says.

Having a best friend would be nice,
but wearing cool clothes, not likely.
I won't be someone's clone.
And that makes me different—uncool.

That and my belly and bra bulge.
I brush a tear from my cheek.
And recall Dante's brief touch.

BETRAYED

Truth is I thought I had a friend.
When we first moved here,
Paige Spoor approached me.

Since she showed interest,
I clung to her like a lifeboat—
acted too needy—new—
desperate for a friend my age.

Couldn't stop my mouth from oversharing.
How was I to know she'd snapped
a photo of the KEEP OUT sign dripping
like a bleeding wall from our trailer?

How was I to know she would Photoshop
a picture of me standing in front of it,
smiling and pointing? How was I
to know she and Abby were frenemies?

Get over yourself.
Move on.
You're not the first person to be used
and abused on Instagram.

ART CLASS

I peek at the black stallion
Dante's painting on his easel—
intriguing—so dark and mysterious.

Dante oozes of lemon, pink pepper,
and cedar—intoxicating cologne.
What is he trying to communicate?
Is he simply completing an assignment?
What symbolism hides in his dark oil image?

He doesn't know I've seen him glance
at the vivid blue Florida scrub jay
drawn on my canvas. *Did I imagine
the almost kiss?*

Could he be interested in me?
Doubt it. I'm too fat.
Is Dante hiding a secret?

What's his story?
He's sleek like the steed—
shy and elusive, but I'm not

stunning like the endangered bird
on my easel, just stuck in my singular
habitat, hiding my secret thoughts,

but planning to learn his story.
What's his secret?

ZACK ATTACK

Although I hate to draw
attention to myself,
my conscience won't allow
me to walk by a Zack attack.

Jamal's surrounded by Zack's wake
of vultures. When Jamal grabs
for his backpack, Zack empties
the contents. Martin
kicks his lunch bag.

An angry fist expands
inside my throat:
"Stop picking on Jamal!
What's wrong with you, Zack?"

Zack laughs, spewing spit.
"Chunk E. Cheese doesn't mind.
Get out of my face, Yankee."

Aha moment. Zack's
resentment stems from
the class debate about
flying the Confederate flag.

The Civil War never ended
in his mind. We're enemies.
                    Ridiculous!

I help Jamal pick up the books
scattered around his feet.
Other than Karol, Jamal's as close
to a friend as I have—a fellow victim.

DON'T BLINK

When I stoop to grab Jamal's book,
Zack plants his foot on the open page,
pinching the edge of my hand.
The odor of socks and weed waft

to my nose. *Athlete smoking?*
Unlike Abby, I don't and won't
kowtow to someone who stinks
from his toes to his brow. Don't

care how many touchdown passes
he's thrown. He's despicable,
and he flaunts his meanness,
daring victims to challenge him.

"Move your foot off my hand."
Our eyes lock and we glare.
Since I refuse to blink first,
Zack shrugs and joins his sidekicks.

As I brush by Zack
and run to class,
my head tells my heart,
"You just made a big mistake."

BLEW IT!

Broke a rule—
my rule.
Zack gave me no choice.

I follow rules—a big difference
between Zack and me.

Broke a rule.
Blurted a stupid comeback.
Lowered myself.

So much is wrong at school,
Something's going to give.
The right action to take is to report
the bully to guidance. I'm weak.

Convince myself I'll step up when Mom
gets home to care for Dad. I'm aware
Mom wouldn't approve of me using
Dad as an excuse. She always says,

"If you don't like how things
are, don't complain. Do something."
Oh, Mom, I can't step up.
I'm a blade of common Bahia grass.

Procrastination's my specialty.
And yet, I just broke my own rule.
Stepped in front of a Mack Truck.

I vow he won't run over me,
and decide to come up with a plan
to deal with the creep. Soon.

ZIT

The rest of my school day—
uneventful except for rain.
No crisis at home either.
I escape to my bedroom early.

Ophelia appears.
I'd like to think
she showed up
because, like a familiar,

she senses I need
her and she wants
to establish a psychic
link. In my dream,
she's made me the human

of her choice.
In the morning
when I stare into
the mirror, I see a zit

the size of a grape,
ripening on top of my nose.
Wrong time of the month
for this to happen.

Is it an omen?

NOTICE ME

After making Dad's breakfast
and cleaning the kitchen,
I rush to the bus and sit
next to Dante with more

hope than usual. Dreamed up a plan
to get inside the greenhouse tonight.

A vein in Dante's forehead twitches.
His face is flushed.
He's obviously in a bad mood.

I want to know why,
but don't dare ask.

Notice me.
I'm not a robot.
I'm not invisible.
I'm not a redneck.

I remember the zit
under the Band-Aid.
Don't notice me.
I look like a Halloween witch.

TEST

Zack blatantly uses
a cell phone app to cheat
during the state exam.
Typical test day.

I tell myself to forget him.
I'm solid third in the class—
ranked below the valedictorian
and salutatorian. Third best—

worse than second best or best,
but not at the bottom, either.
Not my job to police Zack
if he wants to cheat. Keep

to myself. But when we walk
out of the room, he shouts,
"Hey, Riley, if you weren't
such a stupid nobody, you'd know

athletes don't change their socks
when they're on a winning streak.
Stay out of my way, dogface!"
He shoves me aside and storms out.

UNEXPECTED

Surprise. Nobody laughs.
He took too long to respond.
And we lost
more games
than we won.

Last year's homecoming queen
walks by me and whispers
in my ear, "Way to go."

Hmmm.

IMPENDING DOOM?

I walk to the bus, head down,
telling myself Zack's no threat,
but I'm not feeling brave.
Even the name *Zack* makes me sweat.

Mere days to go
before I graduate
and can wave good-bye
to Gertrude Albert High.

Why do I fear I'll never escape?
Will college be different?
Better?

Will I fit in at college?
Yes!

All I want is to get out of here
with a diploma and college
acceptance letter in my bag—

but first I have a mystery
to solve tonight.
I inhale deeply.
No more delays.

OFF GUARD

As I step onto the bus
for the ride home,
I'm thinking about the trap
door. I'm pumped, anxious,

and ready to investigate.
What hides beneath
Dad's greenhouse? *Gotta—*

My chin drops to my chest
when I see Dante rolled
into a protective ball like
a porcupine. His cowered head's

on the duct-taped green vinyl seat,
wedged against the bus window.
But it's too late.
He's already wounded.

A chill inches up my arm—
sensation of a furry centipede
crawls on my bare skin.

No!

AT A LOSS

I slump into the seat.
Dante stares out the window without
glancing my way. I don't blame

him. Someone snipped his man
bun. His hair's been butchered,
cut, and clipped—

Like Samson.

I swallow bile.
How can I lessen

his pain
without calling
attention to how obvious it is?

Or how defenseless
he is?

HOW CAN I HELP?

How?

FUTILE ATTEMPT

After taking a deep
breath, I whisper,
"Wanna talk about it?"

Dante doesn't answer.
I don't push.
We're both powerless.

CLENCHING MY FIST

The bus squeals to a stop.
I can hold back no longer.
Tears roll down my zit-marred
nose as I stomp off the bus,

and charge toward our door.
I hate violence, but if Zack
were here, I'd punch
his smug mug.

I stomp up creaky trailer steps,
clenching my hands into fists.
Over and over I tell myself,
Violence is not the answer.

The door's locked.
"Dad?"

No answer.
I exhale and bruise

my knuckle, punching
the door. Not a smart move.
It's no substitute for Zack's face.

I fish my key out of my bra,
unlock the door, throw my backpack
to the floor and scream.

Is violence the only answer?
I relax my hand.

CAN'T SWALLOW

Blind with tears,
I run to the bathroom.
Throw up—aware
anger can't be flushed

down the toilet like calories.
Not ready to face Dad.
He must be in the greenhouse.

"Thank you, God,"
I whisper as I change clothes.

My mind seesaws from
Dante to the trapdoor.

Pity and curiosity merge
as I wash my face
and brush my teeth
until they bleed.

REGROUPING

The blues harp calls my name.
I stuff it into my pocket.
When I get to the old oak,
I pull it out and blare my inner blues.

Only Ophelia listens. I open
the window to my soul.
For the moment, glad to be alone
with the not-so-stray cat and my

frantic thoughts.

All I see is Dante's sheared bun.
And his struggle to cover his head.
I can't wish or dream it away.
When I open my eyes, the image attacks.

I'm the girl with the weird dad—
the Boo Radley of the sticks.
No chance I can escape my fate.
What gave me false hope?

Dante will never rescue me.
Will I be able to rescue him?
Hope escapes like air from a balloon.
Dante's another doomed mockingbird.
All I see is his jagged haircut.

Almost dead inside, so I close my eyes
and play bluer than blue. No hope left.
Thunder grumbles in the distance.
Clouds threaten to cry inside my head.

Ophelia rubs her back against my leg.
Like a flickering candle,
the flame inside rekindles.
I'm not dead.

MOM NEEDED

Where's Mom?
Why'd she leave the mysterious note?
What's my surprise?
When will she be home?

I need her.
Want advice.
But most pressing,
I want to know
what hides beneath the greenhouse.

Dante and the mystery
of what hides beneath the orchids
keep me from throwing my hands
to the sky in despair.

Does Mom know?
I need to know
what my parents aren't telling me.
What hides beneath the greenhouse?

My quest continues.
But only in my head.
Through the clear greenhouse
plastic, I see Dad in his Boston Red

Sox hat, tending a fragile bloom.
I won't believe he's a survivalist.

OPHELIA

Ophelia appears out of nowhere,
rubs her head against my leg
and yowls. Her eyes penetrate.
Does she know? I bet she does.

Like me, she's curious.
The difference between us—
she has the independence I crave.
I need her, but she doesn't need me.

Without warning, Dad disappears,
teleports like Harry Potter.

CHORES

Before I investigate,
I try to locate Dad.
I head toward the garden,
tackling chores to spend

frustration, planning to pick
vegetables for dinner, but Dad's
in the garden. He points
to a sweet-grass basket with

his hoe and offers a rare smile.
"Saved you some time.
Picked the beans and tomatoes."
He goes back to hoeing.

"Thanks. Dinner will be
ready before six.
Gotta practice reading
a poem for English class."

*Would rather just hand it
in and walk away without
facing Zack and the jocks.*

I don't burden Dad with my problem.
He doesn't need to experience
my crippling fear of standing
in front of a class of jocks

with rivers of sweat dripping down my back.
My voice quivers as it croaks my poem.
I'm a solitary soldier facing a firing squad.

DAD'S WORLD

Dad's so fixed on his task
he doesn't hear or respond.
Mom's right. Horticultural
therapy's cool—the garden
calms Dad and feeds us.

I grab the basket of veggies
and rush to the house.
When I step back outside,
the smell of hamburgers fills the air.

Guess the neighbor up the road
is grilling dinner for his kids.

A burger would be great with tomatoes.
But would it be worth contributing
to global warming?

SHOCKED

I consider myself a cloud watcher,
but I've been so bummed and intent
on gaining access to the trap door, I
haven't glanced at the sky for over an hour.

I'm pacing, trying to think
of an excuse to go
inside the greenhouse when
Dad grabs my hand and says,
"Funnel cloud. Run!"

I turn toward the trailer.
Dad grips my arm and steers
me in a different direction.

Whisks me into the greenhouse,
opens the trap door, and says,
"Head down."

HIDDEN HATCH

The bulkhead hatch slams shut.
We're underground.
Darkness envelops us.
My body quakes, but Dad pulls

a flashlight from an overhead hook.
For once, he's the calm one.
When my eyes adjust to the dim
light, I see cans of food and more

supplies on shelves lining the walls.
"W-where are we, Dad?"

His answer's matter-of-fact.
Like it's totally normal.

"Entrance to our doomsday shelter.
The President has Raven Rock.
We have the Catacombs."

We have the Catacombs?

AFTERMATH

Dad reaches over our heads
and pulls a mattress from a covered
pocket to protect us.
We sit huddled together—

in the bulkhead. It's dark,
but I see an unmarked black door
at the end of the flight of stairs.

Minutes pass like hours.
We don't open the door.
Why?
What's on the other side?

When we surface,
our trailer's standing,
but the roof of our neighbor's
chicken coop is in our yard—

the ultimate trespassing.
"Watch where you step."

I *am* a survivalist's daughter!
But unlike Dorothy,
I have not been swept
off my feet by a raging tornado.

Dad remains remarkably composed,
but we crouch like soldiers
in reconnaissance mode as we
creep toward the trailer.

Good we're looking down.
Our across-the-road neighbor's
charcoal grill lies upside down
in front of our step.

Hot coals smolder,
but the burgers have vanished
in the wind like dandelion parachutes.

NO POWER

Electric wires are broken
puppet strings, dangling
from snapped poles, blocking
the road, but we see our neighbors

looking into the windows
of the now roofless coop.
Dad goes to the fence.
"Everyone okay over there?"

Our neighbor shouts back.
"Yeah, a few chickens
piled on top of each other.
Scared themselves to death.

"We'll get that roof off your
property in the morning.
Those chickens are too scared
to budge tonight."

Dad surprises me.
"Yeah, typical chicken behavior.
I'll give you a hand when you're
ready to carry your roof home."

What's changed?
Early darkness envelops us.
Dad and I follow beams
from his flashlight until
we get inside the trailer.

ACROSS THE TABLE

Since we have no lights,
Dad places a lantern on the table.
We eat peanut butter sandwiches,
tomatoes, cucumbers, and peaches.

A long-ago upstate New York memory
surfaces. Ice storm. Power outage.
Mom served peanut butter
sandwiches, carrot sticks, and apples.

"If the power stays off much longer,
I'll start the generator." Dad
swipes sweat from his forehead.
"Don't want to lose the frozen food."

"We have a generator?"

"Yes, Riley. It's solar powered.
Haven't you seen the panels
in the grid behind the greenhouse?"

I look across the table at my fragile
father with a bit more respect.
It isn't a true Hallmark moment,
but it's good, despite the storm.

For once, I feel safe in the knowledge
Dad's prepared for come what may.
Why didn't I notice the panels?
All I saw was red paint.

TOUCHDOWN

The possibility of a sneak Zack attack
has always weighed on my mind,
but the tornado makes me reconsider.

This touchdown wasn't Zack's.
It prompts me to realize
Zack's not all-powerful.

Dad says, "Mother Nature reminds
us who's boss from time to time."

"Funny, I was just thinking
something like that," I say.

MIDNIGHT GUEST

Rain tap dances on the tin roof.
Like a lullaby, it lulls me to sleep.

A clap of thunder wakes me.
I tiptoe to the living room arch.

Dad's dressed in olive drab.
His rifle points at the door.

He doesn't direct it at me,
but I'm tightrope tense.

When a key turns in the lock,
my heartbeat echoes in my ears.

Mom's no fool. She calls out,
"It's just us. We're home."

Us?

MY SURPRISE

Dad doesn't lower his weapon
until he sees Mom and Gram.

I race into Grams arms like a five-year-
old. "Oh, Gram, you're my surprise.
Thanks for coming for graduation."

"Thank your mom.
I don't drive anymore."

I shrug my shoulders.
"I've never driven."

"Well, it's about time
you learn," Gram says.

She narrows her eyes at Dad,
letting him know she expects
him to teach me.

She's right.
It's time.

How did I think I could escape without driving?
Ride a cloud?
I'm really not a practical person.

Mom says, "Sorry we're late."
She looks me over.

Gram says, "My fault.
I begged her to stop
for the night when the storm—"

RELIEVED

Mom glances at Gram.
"It's just I've never left Riley—"

I've never heard Mom justify
her actions to anyone before.
I hug Mom, inhale her lemon-
basil scent, and glance at Dad.

"Mom, I missed you, but we were fine."

Almost.

When Gram stands to go to bed,
Dad hands his mother a lantern.
"Welcome. Sorry. You'll need this.
I put your suitcase in Riley's closet."

He kisses Gram's forehead,
takes Mom's hand, and leads her
to their room. Gram follows me
into my room with its twin beds.

I'm giggly, but no time to talk.
Gram's tired and falls asleep
as soon as her head touches
the down pillow Mom made

from feathers left over after
Dad shot our Christmas goose.
Mom and Dad believe waste is sin.
We take care of ourselves.

NEED ANSWERS

Lucky for us, or Dad's planning?
We're on the same grid as the fire department.
Whichever it is, our power returns
around one in the morning.

I didn't know.
What else don't I know?

Not knowing drives me crazy.

Will I get an acceptance letter?
Will Dad let me go to college?
Will I ever escape the chains?
Can I break free?

Will I lose weight?
Is it really up to me?

POST TRAUMA

A thud and a clatter
wake me about three.
Gram calls out, "Who fell?"

I stumble out of bed while
Dad steers Mom to a chair.
"Mom, Dad, you okay?"

He's shaking, but she has the bump
forming on her temple. "Watch over
your mother. I'm getting an ice pack."

He takes one step and turns back to face
me. "And don't let her fall asleep."
He kisses Mom's cheek.
"I should move to the Catacombs."

"No!" Mom seizes his arm.
"No harm done. Put a couple
of ice cubes in a washcloth,
and we'll go back to bed."

FLASHBACKS

I had hoped, but even
Gram being here can't
stop Dad's nightmares.

Flashbacks triggered
by what he sees, hears,
or smells take him back

keep him jittery
keep him always alert
keep him on the lookout

for danger. Mom always says,
"Memories bring back the
horrors your father faced."

I close my eyes to forget
the vision of Dante's clipped hair.
My body quivers in fear.

I realize escape is temporary—
fleeting like clouds.

ANSWER

When I was younger,
I avoided asking the
question I needed answered.

After Dad leaves the room,
I blurt out.
"Mom, how many men did Dad kill?"

"Honey, Dad didn't kill.
He saved many soldiers.
As a medic in the Middle East,

"he treated the wounded,
but he can't forget the carnage—
the amputations, the blinded.

"The agony in the faces of those
he couldn't save haunts him.
He watched many men die,

calling for their mothers."

SURROUNDED

I'm in a long, dark hallway
like a cement tomb.
Walls of steel and concrete
surround me.

I smell mold—
the musky, overpowering
odor of patchouli.

I'm fighting, kicking,
breathing frantically,
trying to escape the cocoon
wrapped around my legs.

When I wake in a cold sweat,
my quilt lies in a heap
on the floor. I sit up and scan

my bedroom. Nothing
but a nightmare—

like my life.

Is this what Dad—?

I refuse to go there.

BLACK EYES

In the morning, it's hard
leaving Mom, but she says,
"Hop up, take a shower.
Gram and I will be here when
you get home."

"Mom, you have two black eyes.
I'm afraid to leave you."

"It's all good. Dad had
a nightmare. He kicked,
and I fell out of bed."

"No. It isn't all good."
I shower. No more coconut
shampoo, so I use scent-free.

When I get to the door,
I hug Mom an extra-long time.
"It doesn't feel right leaving you—"

Mom says, "Gram and I will be fine."
Here's your lunch." She hugs me.
"We aren't in danger."

"Dad's helping the neighbor
drag his roof back across
the road, despite—"

She pauses, but my eyes
follow hers to the neighbor's
Confederate flag already flying.
"Your dad's a kind man."

With a combat rifle always within reach.

BROWN BAGGING

I clutch my reusable brown bag.
Mom counts my carbs.
I asked her to do that for me.

Is it my ruse?
Am I scamming her so she
doesn't learn my secret?

Not answering that question.

Why don't I just count carbs?
Or give up bread? Would it help?
Would I drop a few pounds?

Am I my own worst enemy?

As I board the bus, I wonder.
Will Dante come to school today?
Will he speak to me?

Will Dad go off the deep end?
He's kind, but is he sane?
How can Mom be so sure?

Why am I so jumpy?
What do I sense?
Why do I purge?

Why does spine-cooling
dread follow me
down the narrow bus aisle?

ABBY

Abby's cold green eyes glare
at me. As I try to squeeze
by her, she grabs my forearm.
"Dirtbag, how come you've got power?"

I look back at the trailer. For once,
I see Mom's face in the window,
not dribbles of red paint on the front.
"We have a solar generator." I pause.

"Why do you think Dad put
the chains around our property?
We're prepared." I can't
believe my own boasts or lies.

Her unwashed hair sticks to her head.
She reminds me of a wet cat
ready to claw my eyes out.
"Riley, you smell like wet dog."

She pinches her nose.

I say, "Actually, you stink.
You can't substitute
a bottle of patchouli
and incense for soap and water."

As soon as the words
leave my mouth, I'm
embarrassed. How could
I stoop to her catty level?

A memory washes over me—
Abby smells like my nightmare!

DAMAGE

When I sit on the seat next to Dante,
I notice his new haircut.
His man bun's gone, but he looks
fine. If I didn't know ...

Dante stares out the window.
After we pass a car,
wheels up, abandoned in a ditch,
like a roadkill armadillo,

I ask, "Did you have tornado damage?"

"Not personally. A pine tree
landed on my stepfather's car."
He doesn't elaborate,
but isn't rude to me either.

We ride in silence.
I'm shocked by scattered
debris and damage. I see
misery inside and outside the bus.

A carport canopy hangs
from an oak branch.
Reminds me of the last yellow
autumn leaf clinging to a barren

branch before winter sets in.
A nagging feeling I can't
explain shouts *Beware* when I see
a metal gate with a sign painted

in flag red: AGAINST ALL ENEMIES
FOREIGN AND DOMESTIC.
Omen? A stream of sweat dampens
the back of my blouse ...

but Dante spoke to me.
Gotta be a breakthrough?
I regain hope until—

SKETCH

A quick glance at Dante's sketchpad
reveals a 6-D pencil drawing. Drops,
which look like blood,
                         drip,
                              drip,
                                   drip,
from the blade of a knife.

Not good.

I close my eyes to shut out
the scenario it suggests.
When I glance at his sketchpad
again, his clenched fist hides

the drawing on the page,
but not from my mind.
I stare out the window.

All I see is the knife.

Drip,
    Drip,
        Dripping
            Drops
                 Of
                    Blood
                        Scarlet
                             Red
                                BLOOD.

BLINK

Blink, blink, blink.
My eyes open.
Strewn wreckage and downed
trees divert my attention

from Dante's new haircut. I wonder
if he's secretly thankful
for the tornado distraction.

Would I be?
I'm afraid of the answer.

I'm more afraid of Dante's sketch,
the resolve in his face, and the knife
image burned on my retina.

CODE RED.

CLASS ADVISOR

Mrs. González stands outside my homeroom
door, watching what I overheard the substitute
music teacher call *the morning rodeo parade.*
One by one my classmates join what I call

the circle of the included. They
catch up on overnight gossip and plan
parties, sports, and other events.
I won't get an invitation.

The morning ritual mesmerizes me.
Classmates walk up and down the stairs.
The daily march circles, circles, circles.
Cliques—athletes, musicians, nerds,

horse lovers, fern growers' kids, popular girls,
leaders, and followers—enter the circle,
but not Dante. Like me, he lowers his head
and hurries toward his homeroom.

No bonding with friends for us.

Zack sees him and signals to his friends.
I stop in the doorway.
Jocks drop out of the parade and circle Dante.
Mrs. González sees Dante in the middle

of a game of Keep Away.
I hear her vow: "They won't victimize that boy."

BULLY ALERT

"Enough! Split up! Get to homeroom."
Mrs. González enters the circle.

The bullies mumble as they scatter
and slowly shuffle toward their homerooms,
flashing contemptuous smirks at her.

I'm afraid they'll slash her tires or
wait until she's not around to strike
next time—there's always a next time.

FULL MOON

I shiver in the wake of the full moon.
Because of Dad, I know the trouble
the moon brings. That could explain
why I'm anxious, but I doubt it.

I'm afraid Dante's transformed
from pickle in the middle
to formidable foe. Waiting.

Is he carrying a knife like the one
he drew? Will blood flow?
Is he planning revenge?

Am I a traitor if I report what I saw?
It was a sketch, not a knife.
What should I do?

Why am I a magnet for grenades
ready to explode?

WARNING

Charles, the janitor, joins Mrs. González
before she can slip into her room.
I stay still and overhear him say,
"I see things brewing."

"What do you mean?" she asks.

"Threats scratched on stall doors
and more. Scary."

"Please elaborate, Charles,
I have to get to work."

"Crumpled up in wastebaskets
I empty after they go home
are pages those kids find
too private to let slip—

more secrets than they tell.
I read warnings kids toss—
and worse—much worse."

She frowns. "Worse? What do you mean?"

She stares into his eyes, waiting
for his big reveal, and I sigh,
go to my seat—my conscience quieted.
I don't have to betray Dante.

DISCLOSURE

The adults step inside the room.
Charles stands behind my desk and whispers,
"Hair clippings. Brutes cut Dante's hair.
I saw evidence on the locker room floor."

I pretend to read a book.
Mrs. González lowers her voice.
"Oh, no! I noticed his haircut.
Are you going to report it?"

"I think it would be better coming
from a teacher." Charles shifts his weight
and does his *tsk-tsk* to show disapproval.

"Because of the exam schedule,
I'm not free until late in the day.
Do you think it'll happen today?
What are we talking?" she asks.

"Just saying someone needs
to end this horse crap 'cause
I don't care much for mopping
blood off the floor."

"You're right. Better act.
Since Parkland, I don't ignore
any sign of bullying."

The bell rings.
I miss the rest of the conversation.

WAITING FOR JUSTICE

Rumors spread like a virus.
No way Principal Henson can claim
he doesn't know what happened
in the boys' locker room.

All day I wait in vain
for Zack and friends to be
called to the office—
to be arrested or suspended.

Did Dante's mom call the school?
Will Mrs. González talk to guidance?
I can't concentrate on state exams
until Dante gets justice.

But the burrowing toad principal
has dug into his haven and
keeps his head behind closed doors.
Bullies rule the halls.

Why do principals think **it** won't happen here?
Why won't they ask students? We know why
there are so many volcanic eruptions in schools.

ASSUMPTIONS

Was it wrong to assume someone
would do something? Haven't
our administrators heard about
the anti-bullying agenda
or March for Our Lives?

I assumed the vicious attack
on Dante would put a stop
to bullying and wake up our
Gertrude Albert principal.

Wrong! I don't hear a word.
As usual, the disgrace
gets swept under the soiled
carpet, and we walk on it.

Bullies rule this school.
Why is life so unfair?
Why should anyone try?

An inner voice forces me to act.
Wrong to be a bystander.
Don't let evil triumph.
Gotta save Dante.

Between exams, I head to
guidance. Won't—can't sit and wait
for someone else to do something.

BULLETIN BOARD

I stop and look at the bulletin
board with longing.
Oh, the places my classmates
are going!

The board boasts acceptances
for all to see.
I study the counselor's map.

Thumbtacks represent locations
where my classmates plan
to go to college. I ache to place
my green pushpin on that board.

A letter crumpled in my backpack
says I'm wait-listed, standing
on the sideline again,
praying to be accepted.

Ranked in the top percent of the class,
but Dad didn't sign the financial
aid forms on time. Gram
came through with a last-minute

check, so I wait for my slim chance.
Through no fault of my own,
I'm left behind to hope,
trying to squeeze into a spot

away from Gertrude Albert High,
while the jocks ride full boats,
sailing to dream destinations.
"Someone accept me," I whisper.

CAREER THOUGHTS

Vermont State University offers
a minor in writing. Perfect.
I've read enough to know
poetry won't pay the bills.

I plan to get my degree
in ecology and environmental ethics
and minor in writing.
Earth Day is my birthday.

But I fear Dad
will keep me within our chain-linked
confines, so he can protect me
from outsiders—not what I want.

I want to be free to roam
like Ophelia. But right now my mission
is to report and stop Zack's bullying.
No time for lingering.

GUIDANCE

At the office door I stop,
take a deep breath,
approach the guidance secretary,
"May I please speak to Mr. Bern?"

Since his door's open,
Mr. Bern sees me, smiles,
and motions to a chair.
"Have you received a college
acceptance? How can I help you?"

"No. I'm wait-listed."

"Don't worry you'll get in."

"That's not why—"
I stop. Start over.
"Could you stop Zack?"

"Stop Zack?"
He smiles as if it's all good.
Straightens papers on his desk.

"What did Zack do now?
He likes to mess around. Boys
will be boys, and he's a jock."

"No! Zack's brutal and degrading.
He and his wingmen cut
Dante's hair. His
endless harassment hurts—"

MELTDOWN

Mr. Bern smiles. Attempts
to calm me. "You're too sensitive.
Dante's hair will grow back.
I saw him this morning."

My face must register shock,
because he adds,
"Dante looks fine. Don't
take teasing so seriously."

*What? Does he see me as a toddler
he can offer a pacifier?*

I melt down in his office.
My mouth is a raging flood,
sucking up caution in its path.

Anger tears roll down my cheeks—
unrestrained—like Zack and Martin.

"Mr. Bern, it's more than teasing.
It's demoralizing. Doesn't the school
want to keep all students safe?
How can *you* of all people tolerate
cruelty and bigotry?" I grit my teeth.

"Boys will be boys. Really? The best excuse
you can offer? How can you justify bullying?"
I lick my salty lips—disheartened, spent, defeated.

"Riley, it's just a little senioritis."

I step closer to his desk. "Not how I see it."

What a sad excuse for a guidance counselor.

FUMING

I reach for a tissue, regrouping.
Mr. Bern's response makes me
feel as if I'm beating my head
against a concrete wall.

Inhale. Exhale.

So far,
I'm lousy in the activist role.
But I won't be appeased.
Not today.

Not anymore.

"Coaches and jocks wield
too much power! Why does everybody
in school and town cave to a pigskin?
Where are the adults in this place?"

I storm out of guidance and collide
smack into Mrs. González. "Sorry," I mumble.
"Good luck. I can't get him to understand."

But somehow as I stomp away spent,
the fire I saw in Mrs. González's eyes
revives hope. I inhale and head to chorus—
conscience clear. She's got this.

She'll make Mr. Bern deal with Zack.
If she doesn't, I'll talk to the security officer.

GOWNS AND TASSELS

A voice over the intercom calls
seniors to the auditorium
to try on mortarboards.
Tassels swish like ponytails.

Mrs. González, our pudgy advisor,
wasn't kidding when she told Charles
she had a busy day ahead of her.

She hands out gowns, "Press these so you'll
be presentable to walk across the stage."

When she says, "We're going
to do a practice, lining up in the order
you'll enter next Friday night," I panic.

What if no one will walk with me?

Fate intervenes. Karol and I
are the same height and will march
in side by side. Karol doesn't make a fuss.

Phew!

BOLD MOVE

Our class president leads a chant:
"Almost out of here.
Nothing left to fear.
The end of high school is near."

On the way out the door,
Zack elbows me.
"Is that the first new
thing you've ever worn?"

"At least, I don't stink like
yesterday's pizza," I say before
I take time to think it through.
"Do you ever change your socks?"

I don't regret my snarky
remark. I know it was dumb
to say it, but I like the spark
I see in Dante's eyes.

Later, when Karol passes me in the
hall, she whispers, "Wish I
had half of your courage."

DINNER CONVERSATION

Since Gram's visiting and
the sight of Dante's haircut
is so disturbing, I rush
home to the shiny trailer.

Mom made a delicious
vegetable lasagna and salad,
but Gram's blueberry cobbler
steals the spotlight.

When the conversation turns
to school, I unload my troubles.
"Why won't the school stop
the bullying?" I ask.

Mom's answer stuns me.
"Some people have tied
the bullying agenda to gay
rights. They claim
it's an un-Christian—"

Gram says, "Honey, some conspiracy
theorists deny Sandy Hook happened."

I slam my palm on the table
"That's just crazy!"

WRONG

The plates rattle a response.
"Neither Dante nor Jamal

are gay, and they're the
victims at Gertrude Albert.
Bullies cut Dante's hair."

I don't tell my family I'm the
log of stool in the school pool.
That's too personal,

but Dad winces. I've ruined
our quiet family dinner.
Wrong time to vent?

Never right to vent
in our home.

But Dad surprises me.
He turns to Mom.

UNCOVERED

"Make a call, Leyvi. Find
out what's going on at that
school before I go and do
some head-shaving of my own."

I get up planning to run
to the bathroom, but Mom
holds me back. We lock eyes.
She's in full-Mom mode.

"Please show me your knuckles."

She inspects me like a mother
cow checks her newborn calf.
What is she looking for?
What does she suspect?

Mom excuses herself and goes
to call the school.
But I don't hear her conversation.

WHAT HIDES BENEATH

My confused grandmother
says, "Ian, show me your garden."

I assume Gram plans to defuse
the grenade that is my dad.

I follow them out the door,
wishing, but doubting an orchid
will calm the fire inside me.

Like a sunflower drawn to the sun,
I'm pulled to what hides beneath Dad's
greenhouse sanctuary. I eavesdrop.

"If the stairs won't be too much for you,
I'll take you to the shelter I've restored.
You'll be amazed."

I've never heard such enthusiasm
in Dad's voice before.
He so excited to show his mother,
he doesn't see me tailing Gram.

Grooves form between Gram's brows.
"The shelter?"

CONCERN

"Think, *Alas, Babylon.* I refurbished
a huge underground fallout shelter—
the largest privately-owned bomb shelter
in the nation," Dad says.

"Used to be called the Catacombs."

I stare, shocked, still
when he opens the hatch door.
"Built around the Kennedy's Cuban
missile crisis to house the mayor
and this town's bigwigs."

Gram takes Dad's hand. "Oh, honey."
She reaches up to kiss his cheek
"You still fear a nuclear war?"

"More than ever, Mom.
I must protect my family.
Come on inside."

He takes her arm to lead her down
the steep set of stairs.

It seemed so small.
How did I miss ....

SECRETS

I step out from behind Gram.
"May I see, too, Dad?
You never showed me
whatever's beyond the door."

He hesitates. Shrugs.
"Yeah, I guess you're old
enough to keep a secret."

He has no idea how many secrets
I'm keeping, especially the knife.
Should I have told Mr. Bern?

Would Mom have told Mr. Bern?

UNDERGROUND

Dad, Gram, and I inch our way
through the eerie darkness with only
Dad's lantern lighting the stairs.
We reach the steel door.

When he pulls the door open,
and hits the light switch, Gram and I
gasp in disbelief. Wow!

Gram says, "Ian, this is an underground city."

"Not quite, but a hundred people
could hunker down for more than a year.
Since it was designed for twenty-five
families, we can rest assured—"

"But so many weapons," Gram says,
wiping sweat from her forehead.

The arsenal shocks me, too.
We could go to the war
Dad wages in his head
and win. Unsettling.

Dad points to a wall.
"We've stocked a selection
of heirloom seeds." He points
to another room.

"In there we have topsoil.
We can be self-sufficient for years."

And buried alive under radioactive orchids!

OVERWHELMED

We pass six bathrooms,
ten showers, a few kitchens,
canned foods, freeze-dried
foods, medicines,
and a stationary bicycle.

"What's the bicycle for?" I ask.

"To run the blower for the
air-conditioning system in
an emergency."

"Not what I pictured,"
Gram and I say simultaneously.

"With luck, it's not what anyone pictures.
I don't want interlopers. I'd rather not
ever have to use a weapon again."

Doesn't make sense.
He spends hours shooting
bottles off fence posts out back.

"If there's a war,
and we're forced to stay here,
could I at least bring Ophelia?"
I hear the whine
in my voice when I plead.

"The stray cat?"
I nod. He shrugs.
"Sure. Get some supplies at the Dollar Tree."

Who is this man I call Dad?

He's like summer rain—unpredictable.

WHAT I DIDN'T ASK

Sure.
I want to keep Ophelia.
I'd need company to cuddle
at night in the Catacombs.

But
Dante is the one I want
to save.

There.

I've said it,
in my mind.

But

I didn't ask Dad,

or Mom,
or even Gram
if I could invite him.

Why?

Do I fear he won't accept me?
Maybe, he'd rather die
than be stuck in a bunker
with me.

I shiver at the thought
of living underground,
but ... *What if?*

5,000 SQUARE FEET

"Was the town small enough
for the Catacombs to hold
all the residents?" I ask.

"No, Riley." Dad sighs.
"The plan was for the mayor,
the superintendent of schools,
a couple of doctors—"

"The wealthy." Gram waves
a hand in disgust.

I'm shocked. I've never seen her angry.
Her cheeks turn the color of a plum.

"Bet not one official spent a day
on the battlefield." She looks
to Dad for an answer.

He shrugs. "The twenty-five wealthiest
families. You draw your own conclusion."

"Revolting." Gram's mouth tightens.

I'm intrigued.
Want to know more.
But Gram's tired. She needs
to go back to the trailer.

How did I miss this?
Why didn't I ask to see
where the door led?

Why don't I ask questions?
Am I afraid of the answers?

A SONG

As we walk toward our trailer,
Dad says, "The Catacombs
were built fifty years ago
and abandoned, until I heard
about the property and bought it
for a song—"

"What's that mean?" I ask.
"A lot or a little?"

"For what we have, a little.
The walls are a foot thick,
but keep in mind when I
purchased the shelter,
it didn't look like it does now."

He shakes his head. "Most people
wouldn't have stepped inside to save
their lives. But I don't trust North Korea."

"Why?" I ask.

"Their missile tests."

I nod.

"What did it look like when we came?"

I'm asking questions now.

DAD'S RESTORATION

Dad closes his eyes
for a couple of seconds.

"It was an eyesore, teeming
with roaches. Rust and mildew
covered machines and supplies.
Otherwise, we wouldn't own it."

"We couldn't have afforded
it in mint condition."
He's animated. "But I had a vision."

"If people knew what I've done here,
it could become dangerous for us
during a national emergency.

You understand, Riley?
It could mean life or death."

"Yes, I understand."

But I'm not sure I do.

I'm anxious.
My body shudders.

We return to the greenhouse.
As we amble through the orchids,
Gram says, "What hides beneath
kinda scares me, son. Taints the beauty."

"We must prepare for the future.
This should put your mind at ease, Mom.
So, I don't have to worry.
It's why I want you to move here."

"And sell my home? I couldn't.
Your dad built my house.
I promised him on his deathbed
I'd never sell it.
Besides I cannot leave the boat."

The color bleaches from Dad's face.

BOAT?

Another secret.
What boat?
Did I see it?

Something shared between them
unsettles us.

We trudge uphill
the long walk through
the orange grove
to the Airstream, each of us
in a singular troubled world.

Together, but apart.
Like Dante and I
on the school bus seat.

Lonely.
Scared.
Hurt.
Regretful.

Hopeful?

I have to tell Mr. Bern about the knife.

Everyone will call me Snitch,
especially Dante.

A tear rolls to a stop on my nose.
Like a zit.

WARNING

Dad stays silent the rest of the night.
His mind goes wherever it goes
when he leaves the present.

Neither Mom nor Gram reach him.
Gram watches him like a mama bear.

She realizes she's cocked the trigger.

When we get to my room,
Gram seems to need to talk.
She asks, "Do you have a boyfriend?"

"No. I kinda like a guy, but—"

"But what?"

"He keeps to himself.
Barely knows I exist.
He's very quiet."

"Well, you be careful, Riley.
My grandmother always
said, 'Still waters run deep.' "

I want to ask what she means,
but she turns toward the wall,
and falls asleep, leaving me
to think over her warning.

FIND

I make Gram's bed in the morning.
A poem on yellow-lined paper appears
to have fallen from her *Holy Bible* to the floor.
I can't resist the urge to read it.

After reading it, I wonder.
How long ago did she write this?

Maybe she meant for me to read it.
Why?

Whether or not I was meant to do so,
I read it. Again. And again.

EPISTLE TO A LOST SON

I visited the War Museum last night.
Tucked away in a corner, a small table
Covered by a linen cloth, pure white,
Made my knees, like a volcano, unstable.

Dormant memories surfaced in the dim light.
The empty chair reminded me of the price you paid
When your plane went down mid-flight.
I can't forget the sacrifice for freedom you made.

All contact lost, so Dad and I were left to wait.
For too many weeks, we shed silent tears
While waiting—waiting for word of your fate.
Salt sprinkled on a plate, lest we forget the fears.

Your portrait over the piano. Your room, as you left it.
The boat you built shrink wrapped in the backyard.
Inside the house, the furniture you and Dad crafted.
For Dad and me, to lead a normal life became too hard.

On the table, a slice of lemon on a white plate signifies
Your fate was bitter one weather-doomed flight.
We knew you didn't vaporize into the skies,
But your aircraft disappeared from radar sight.

Missing—a frozen mountain near Kabul hid the crash site.
On the table, for your bravery, a red rose rests ...
While I stood near the candle, reminiscent of your bright light,
I recalled your sacrifice, a soldier's bequest.

At last, experts identified your remains, using my DNA.
Still in your empty chair, no others dare sit.
The inverted wineglass symbolizes you cannot toast.
But rest proud, son, of your heroism the table boasts.

THE REST OF THE POEM

The rest of the poem
appears on the back of the page,
stained with teardrops:

Wives and mothers know war isn't a game.
In the end, Riley, you didn't come home to play ball.
Your brother's burdened with survivor's guilt and isn't the same.
He bans excuses, so his daughter can't grasp her dad's pain at all.

Heads hang morning-fog low when the brave fall.
But who will help the traumatized the latest war built?
Before he passed, Dad and I buried one hero son with a baseball.
Our surviving son hides behind a chain-link fence built by guilt.

INHERITANCE

When I finish reading Gram's
poem, I sit on the bed and sob.
It helps me get Dad, but …

so sad and shocking. Poor Gram.

A tremor shakes my core.
I never realized the extent
of the responsibility I've inherited.

Weighty being named for Dad's
dead brother—a hero.

I need to grow a spine.

And poor guilt-ridden Dad.

Why do survivors feel guilty?
Isn't survival life's goal?
Didn't people embrace
Darwin's *On the Origin of Species?*

Life's both a mystery,
and a game of roulette.

Dad's merely prepared.
He isn't a militant.

STEP FORWARD?

The sound of a hammer says Dad's
up early pounding. From my window,
I see stakes and Dad positioning
boards, forming a wooden rectangle.

No time to investigate why.
Today's different. I'm clutching
Gram's poem and staring
straight ahead when I take

the usual seat on the bus.
After a minute, Dante speaks,
"Sup?" His voice is so soft
I wonder if he actually spoke,

or if I'm imagining it. But he
stretches his neck.
"What are you guarding?"
He leans toward the poem.

"A coded message?
A purloined letter?" He laughs.
"Your spoken-word poem?
"A love note?" he asks.

Do I detect jealousy?

SCARY CONVERSATION

My voice trembles when I answer.
"It's a tribute poem."

"Did you write it for class?
You like to write poetry?"

"No. Well, yes, but I didn't write this."

"Who did? What's it about?"
He's never shown so much interest.

Is he the calm before a storm?

"My grandmother. Sh-she's visiting
until graduation." I cover my mouth.
I fear I've revealed too much.

He pushes me for more.

REVELATION

"I don't understand one line,
and I want to ask Mrs. González
what to do. I'm undecided."

"About what?"

I don't want them to,
but the words escape.

"I've been praying to get
out of here for—forever. My dad's
made me an outcast with his
chain-link fence and KEEP

OUT drizzled on the trailer,
but now I understand why,
and I think he plans to build
our forever home here."

I snap my mouth shut
like a bear trap.
Conversation over.

Why did I tell him?
Why did he ask?
Have things changed between us?

Are our stars aligned?

"Still waters run deep."

ENGLISH CLASS

I love Mrs. González, but she's right to retire.
She got this bright idea for the oral section
of our final to be spoken-word poetry.

*Why not just put me in front
of a firing squad and end my misery?*

I've been working on writing a new poem
because my usual poems would alienate me
further, but writing on command—not me.

Mrs. González unleashed my
classmates. Spoken-word poems morph
to mean-spirited insult poems.

I love poetry, but hate sharing
my poems aloud. I'm no Amanda Gorman.
Like Emily Dickinson,
I keep my poems unseen in my room.

Did Mrs. González plan for our poems
to diffuse hostility? 'Cause all
these poems do is create anxiety.

Abby slams misfits like me.
She's all bubbly and smug
as she returns to her seat.

Mrs. González gasps.
Her face turns ruby red.
No question she realizes
she's made a mistake.

Put a bullet in the chamber.

TRAPPED

God, I need to get out of here.
But I know it's too late.
The mousetrap is set.
I suspect I'm about to eat the cheese.

Zack Hickson struts
to the front of the room.
I've disarmed a man—faced
a weapon of war, but I fear his poem.

Hold my breath.

QUARTERBACK ATTITUDE

But Zack rests his elbows
on the lectern and laughs.

"Like whatev.
Maybe, tomorrow
I'll hand in a limerick.
Being quarterback tops
passing this class."

Zack swaggers to his seat,
snaps a piece of lined paper
against his hip.

Phew! I've escaped his bullet.

I exhale in relief—too soon?

TROUBLE'S BREWING

Karol's next.
She sobs and runs from the room
because Zack oinks when she walks
by him. I'm not sure if Mrs. González

heard him, but maybe she did.
She says, "Zack, see me after class."

She calls on Dante when Karol returns.
Dante's words—"Live by the blade.
Die by the knife" would scare Hannibal Lecter.

His final maniacal laugh shuts
Zack down for the rest of the day.

My hand covers my mouth,
stifling a gasp. My shoulders tighten
when I see Mrs. González look my way.

"Still waters run deep" echoes.

Beads of sweat form under my armpits.
Rivulets run down my sides.
"Riley Barrie," Mrs. González says.

My head's a spinning Disney teacup.
In my woozy head, the class
turns to a Mad Tea Party ride.

I'M THE GOOSE

Goose.
I rise, feeling tagged
like a kid in Duck, Duck, Goose.

I'm overwhelmed by the day's events—
beginning with my morning conversation
with Dante and ending with his poem.

Knees shaking, palms sweating,
I stand to deliver my poem,
but I'm choking back tears.

Until this moment, I've
considered poems friends
that won't walk away from me,
but today's different.

My words sputter and vaporize.
I totally bomb the assignment—
squeeze out a four-stanzas pantoum,
and return to my seat,

shaking—face hot
as a cast-iron pancake griddle.

Stage fright or something scarier?
Why am I so jittery today?
Typical ineffective me?

Or something more? Clairvoyance?

NIGHTMARE

In my nightmare, Zack bullies
me into accepting wrongs.
In my nightmare, I am satisfied
attending a sexist school.

In my dreams, I am horticulturist
and poet Emily Dickinson, living
a solitary life in a dandelion-yellow
house near the town cemetery.

A common thread—
fear—
mesmerizing and isolating.

Karol fears Zack.
Dad fears Armageddon.
Gram and I fear Dad will detonate.

I fear a knife,
drenched in blood,
drawn in Dante's sketchbook.

Drip.
    Plop.
        Splat.

FEAR

Fear leads to threats, conflicts,
and renewed interest in bomb shelters.

My newest secret, the Catacombs,
hidden beneath Dad's orchids.

Ending up in the bunker—
my greatest fear.

Mom fears nothing.

What's her secret?
I need Mom's courage.

UNCHARACTERISTIC ACT

Calculus class anomaly draws
my attention to Zack. Slyly,
he slips an envelope
with the words *banquet tickets*

scribbled on top into a book
on the team manager's desk.
He jabs Matthew's shoulder
playfully with his fist.

Since Matthew's desk
is right in front of mine,
I overhear their conversation.

"Sorry about your dad's
accident, Bud. If you need
anything let me know."

Matthew looks at Zack
with worshipful eyes,
"Thanks, Zack. You're the best."

"Look, Bud, you and your girl
sit with the team at the banquet."

Wow!
Zack exhibited a shred of decency.

EXPECTATIONS

Performance poetry assignment
over without apparent repercussions.
Was Mrs. González right?

Did we just need to vent?
Did I ruin my grade?
I search the outline to see if she

said the oral portion of the final
exam counted for ten or twenty
points. The rubric says ten. *Yay.*

Later, Dante and I ride home
on the loud bus without conversation.
Enough exposure for one week.

We sit comforted
by shared silence.
And no expectations.

MAIL

After school,
I go to the mailbox praying.
PLEASE, GOD, let me escape
high school, chain-link fences,
and scary secrets.

And it's there—
an envelope with the return
address I've waited for.
Hands trembling—I tear open,
the bulky packet.

Is it my ticket out of here?
Will I be able to leave?

I clutch the letter.
Hands clammy—eyes
seek the prayed-for

word on the page.
Fearing it's a formal rejection,
I scan the lines.

"I am pleased to congratulate
you on your acceptance into ...

"Yes!"

I dance around the mailbox.
Pumping one empty fist
over my head, waving the letter
like a parade flag in the other hand.

Yes!
Yes!
Yes!

I'm ACCEPTED—finally.
Accepted.
Life Changing.

I tuck the letter in my cleavage
and hand Mom the rest of the mail.
How will I approach Dad with the news?

ANOTHER CHALLENGE

I'm still lightheaded when Dad
surprises me. "Come on,
Riley, time for a driving
lesson. You ready?"

"Yes. Where will we go?"

"We'll start on the dirt
road behind the greenhouse."

Phew!

I'm afraid to drive on a busy
Florida highway. More afraid
to tell him about the letter.

I give Dad a bumpy ride.
He says, "Good first time
behind the wheel."

NERVOUS

All night I'm water bubbles
dancing on a hot griddle.
When Gram and I get to my room,
I show her the letter. "Should I go?"

She asks, "Why wouldn't you go?"

"I'm afraid to leave Mom
alone with Dad."

She hugs me. "You owe it to
yourself. Go! Live your life."

"Really? Would it be selfish?"

"No, it's natural to want
your independence, but—"
She stops mid-sentence.

"What were you going to say?"

"Well, Riley, you may not want
to hear it, but you hated the cold.
Cried your toes were freezing
when your mom took you skating."

"I forgot about that."

"Make sure you aren't running
'away from'. Run 'to' something."

Gram says, "I'm sure you recall
vacations on Lake Champlain
with your mom's family. They adored you,
but –" She stops switches directions.

"Go talk to your parents."

WORDS I'LL EAT

"I don't care if the school
blows up tomorrow.
I'm accepted into college.
Let my new life begin."

I kiss Gram's cheek.
Hug Ophelia too hard.
The little gray ball of fur flees my grip.
Runs to hide under the bed.

Ophelia reminds me too much
attention threatens her independence.
And mine.

I don't own her,
But I'd like to think she
knows we need each other.

"I don't care about the dumb banquet."

That's a lie.
Secretly, I care.
I wanted Dante to invite me.

I had hope.

But I got what I wanted most,
didn't I?

I run to my parents' bedroom,
knock on the door, and share
my acceptance letter with them.

BACK IN MY ROOM

"I have a question, Gram."

She smiles. "Hope I have an answer.
Did it go well with your parents?"

"Okay. I think ... what's the boat like?"

She doesn't ask which boat.
She knows I mean Uncle Riley's boat.

I hear resignation in her voice.
I've trod on a thorn.
"What do you want to know about it?"

"What kind of boat was it?"

She gets a faraway look.
"A yellow shanty boat.
Houseboat—complete with dingy.
Has a green hull and a porch."

She pulls a 4x7 photo album
out of her suitcase. "The little window
box was designed to make it look
like a small floating cottage on the lake,
but it never made it to the boat ramp."

"Why?"

Why did I ask? I know I don't want the answer.

"Because the day he chose for the maiden voyage,
Riley got his orders to report for duty. He never put
the boat in the water. No one ever has.
Gramps encased it in shrink wrap after—

BREATHING IN

I hug Gram and say,
"Maybe, we should take it out next spring—
Otherwise his work would be in vain."

Sort of a Titanic disaster without going to sea.

Her answer is slow to come.
Gives me time to close my eyes
and recall a shape covered in ghost
white plastic—the boat never
moved from her backyard.

"Yes, Riley, someone should see if it floats.
Who better to take it out than his namesake?"

Gram shows me a picture of Uncle Riley
standing in front of the shanty boat.
"You have his beautiful gray eyes
and wheat blonde hair." She

brings me to her chest and hugs
me—no clings to me—reminding
me of how I squeeze Mom
to me after a Dad meltdown,
breathing in her strength.

Is Gram inhaling my scent
the way I breathe in Mom's?
Does she hope I smell like him?

DREAMS

"Realize his dream," Gram says.

"I read your epistle to Uncle Riley.
Didn't get,
'Salt sprinkled on a plate,
lest we forget the fears.'"

"It refers to one of the symbols I saw
on the Fallen Comrade Table
at the War Museum. The table would
humble any Gold Star Mother.

"My son's spirit lives in my broken heart."

Her sobs stop my probing.
No more questions tonight.
How will I ever fall asleep?

I'm a walking mirror of a dead man.
Never realized I stole his looks
as well as his name.

"I think his spirit lives in Dad's heart too."

Does seeing me bring on Dad's—
I can't go there.
That would be too awful.

If I trigger his flashbacks,
my leaving will be a godsend for him.

OPHELIA

As soon as my head hits the pillow,
Ophelia comes out from under the bed
and bolts for the door.

She meows until I get up
and let her out. Ophelia makes
sure I know she's an outdoor cat—

doesn't like to be handled,
prefers little or no human contact.
I don't own her. No one does.

She won't come back
until she's hungry again.
I've broken our contract.

Have I hung the wrong name on her?
She's wants independence.
Is that really what I want?

I'm forced to self-hug, but
too optimistic to care.

In the middle of the night, a memory
wakes me. I sit up in bed, recalling
the shrink-wrapped boat and trailer,

and Gramps saying, "Don't
climb up on the boat. You'll fall."

Sleep's a long time returning.

OPHELIA RETURNS

Ophelia's beneath my window,
whimpering. Frantic, I run
outside, scoop her up and rush
her to Dad. "Dad, something's

wrong with Ophelia. She cries
when I touch her leg. Can you help?"

He takes her from my arms.
Gently, he examines her.
"Looks like a BB grazed
her left leg." He cleans

and bandages the wound.
"She'll walk fine in a day or two.
Lucky. Since the BB didn't lodge
in her leg, she won't need surgery.

The bandage will keep her from licking
the spot. Don't let her roam."

She limps when she tries to walk.
I feel awful. Whether she a stray
or feral cat, captivity won't sit well

with my independent friend.
Yet, roaming wild endangers her.
Forces me to question my motives.

Did I wish dependency on her?
I wanted to feel needed—
my insecurity is not pretty.

CAN'T CATCH A BREAK

I better understand Ophelia
as I place her in a makeshift
bed, wipe tears from my cheek,
and run to catch the bus.

Mr. Robert Frost, you're wrong.
The bright yellow of the sun,
not gold, is earth's hardest
hue to hold. I dare to argue

with America's celebrated
and admired poet because
I can't catch a break. On the bus,
Dante's cracking his knuckles.

Beads of sweat line his forehead.
He mumbles something about
Eddy the sweaty.
His aura gives the impression

something's wrong—terribly wrong.
Why is he avoiding eye contact?
I try to get him to talk.
"Who's Eddy the sweaty?"

"The creep my mother married
when Dad bailed after—"

He clams up.
Stares out the window.
No breakthrough.

So I study the other riders.
Did one of them shoot Ophelia?
Fear, doubt, and uncertainty
accompany me to school.

Not going there today.
When we get to school,
despite this morning's events,

I'm excited to put my pushpin
on the bulletin board.
I'm going to make it.

Only eight days to go.

WRONG

I jinxed myself with my enthusiasm.
A scribbled note tacked on the board
scares me, makes me swear:

"EVER HEARD 'HIS LUCK RAN OUT'?
ZACK AND MARTIN BETTER COOL IT.
DANTE'S A TIME BOMB. TICK TOCK."

Who wrote that?

Did Paige Spoor plant that so she
can put it in her sleazy column?
No. Her aunt, the newspaper advisor,
would edit it out.

I don't see Bubba, the prom king,
glancing over my shoulder. He startles
me when he says, "Way to go.
Great skiing in Vermont."

He raises his hand,
and we high-five each other.
Didn't see that coming/

A little late, but I'm gaining
acceptance at Gertrude Albert,
and I'm liking more classmates.

If Ophelia weren't home, injured
and Dante weren't in a snit,
I'd be flying high. It ...

SYSTEM OVERLOAD

At lunchtime, I grab my brown bag
from my locker. I'm hungry
and hopeful when I enter the cafeteria.

Dante steps out from behind
the accordion room separator.
I freeze when he points a revolver

at Zack's zipper, and glances at me.
His eyes are as riveting
as the gun in his shaking hand.

The air rushes out of the room.

"I like you the way you are.
Don't ever change to fit a mold.
This one's for you, Riley," he says,

and shoots Zack. I scream.
Stare shocked-still. Blood stains
Zack's pants. He drops to his knees,
begs, "Please. No."

With seconds remaining
on the quarterback's clock,
Dante aims the second round
between Zack's eyes.

He shoots. Spins.
Coach runs to cradle Zack.
He stares at the gun, frozen.

Dante directs the next round at Martin.
When Martin faints,
Dante taunts Coach. "Isn't this fun?"

BULLETS FLY

Before Coach can answer,
Dante points the gun
at the teacher's chest.
The gun fails to feed.

Dante adjusts his grip.
Abby's screams divert his attention
to her, instead of Coach.

"Wear this to the senior banquet."
he yells and cocks his gun.

I elbow his arm.
Confusion follows.
Somehow a bullet grazes my arm,
splattering my blood, the color
of Abby's shiny nail polish,
onto her dress.

SMITH & WESSON

Chaos.
Random scattershot
followed by my piercing screams.

When Dante points the Smith
& Wesson at Mr. Bern, I shout,
"Dante, stop."

My classmates panic, run,
hide under tables.
Their eyes wide with shock
and fear. My eyes lock with Dante's.

"Drop the gun, Dante. Please."

Beads of sweat shine on his lip.
Blood drips from my arm.
He redirects the barrel at Abby.

I don't know why, but I step
toward him, grab his wrist—
as if I haven't heard about what happened
to the seventeen in Parkland ...

BLOOD

Dante wrenches free.
Presses the revolver
against his ear and pulls
the trigger. Blood splatters

Everywhere

Blood

My tongue swipes
the corner of my lip.
I taste iron, but I see

black.

As I regain consciousness,
I hear sirens wailing.

Or is it me screaming?

"Mom, I tried," I whisper.
I close my eyes—

I don't want to see or hear.

Blood.
Blood—
tastes like iron.

I've seen too much—like Dad.
I don't want to open my eyes.
But I do.

STRETCHER

Splatters of gray matter
and blood cover my clothes—
Dante's brains and blood.

I faint again.
This time I'm being
carried on a stretcher
when I awake.

I try to get up.
"I'm okay,"
I say.

But I'm not.

How could I be?

EMT

A gentle EMT looks
into my eyes before
placing an oxygen mask
over my nose and mouth.

I recognize pain in his eyes.
Pain like I've seen in Dad's eyes—
not easy being a first responder.

That's one truth I witness daily.

HOSPITAL

Hours later I open my eyes.
I know it's late because
the curtain on the hospital

window is open. Except
for the full moon, it's black
as soot outside. I shiver.

Close my eyes.
Please, let me wake
from this nightmare.

But the terrors
are just beginning.

TEARS

I wake to the overpowering,
sanitizer smell of hospital.
I'm living my worst nightmare.

Dad paces back and forth.
Mom leans over and kisses
my temple. "Oh, my baby."

When salty warm tears stream
down my cheeks, Gram pulls
a tissue from her sweater sleeve.
"That's good, honey, let the tears flow."

*How did I let myself
get lulled into believing my life
was on the upswing?*

A policeman steps forward.
"If you're awake, I have a
few questions for you."

MY PROTECTOR

Dad says, "Not now."
To shield me, he steps between
my bed and the policeman.

He's the medic, caring for the wounded.

Again.

"It's all right, Dad.
Let me get the questions over with
so we can go home."

Dad steps away from my bed,
but stays in the room.

QUESTIONS

"Before I answer any questions,
are Zack and Dante dead?"

The cop says, "Dante killed
Zack and himself.
Now I have questions for you."

"Fire away." I put my hand
over my mouth. "But you'd
be better off questioning the other bullies.
Just saying."

"Aren't they traumatized enough?"
His tone of voice says the cop's furious.
He thinks I'm an accomplice—
at best—a hostile witness.

How could I have been so wrong?

LAWYER

Gram says, "Ian, let me hire a lawyer."

I put my hand up. "Don't
waste your money, Gram.
I didn't do anything wrong."

But the police think I did.

As soon as the questions begin,
Mom says, "Don't answer until
we hire a lawyer."

"I don't need a lawyer. I'll answer."

I need Gram to save her money for college.

"This is ridiculous." I sob.
"I didn't know."

NOT MY BOYFRIEND

Dad's on high alert.
Moves to the opposite side
of my bed from the cop.
Watches him.

The opening questions seem harmless.
"What's your full name?"

"Riley Gertrude Barrie."

"Gertrude?"

The way he says my middle
name makes me explain.
"Mom loves Shakespeare, especially *Hamlet.*"

He nods his head. "How long have you
been sharing a seat on the bus
with your boyfriend, Dante?"

"Whoa! Boyfriend?"

CLARIFYING

"He's not my boyfriend."
I pause, waiting for the next question,
but it doesn't come, so I answer.
"Since he moved here."

"You've been sitting next to him
daily, but he isn't your boyfriend?"

"We're the two loners. Pariahs.
I've never had a boyfriend."

Wow! It hurts.
Wish Gram and my parents
hadn't heard my answer.

INTERROGATION

The cop's badge reads *Sergeant Goodfellow.*
He asks, "How long have you
and Dante been planning a massacre?"

"I-I didn't know he was going to shoot anyone."

"You expect me to believe you sat next to him
on the bus and didn't know of his plot?"

"I-I don't expect you to believe anything,
but the truth. I didn't even know he owned
a gun. Never saw it before—"

Why won't my hands stop trembling?

Should I tell him about the drawing of the knife?
Should I have questioned Dante about it?

Knowledge of the knife
is gnawing on my conscience,
but the policeman's attitude
makes me grind my teeth.

In my confused mind, his attitude
justifies my reluctance to spill
my guts unless he asks
the right questions.

"What did Dante tell you?"

He doesn't just ask questions.
He demands answers.
His attitude infuriates me.

My head pounds.

TRUTH

I answer truthfully. "Nothing."

Two can play the Sergeant's game.
I'm afraid. But don't elaborate.

He gets in my face.
"Then why'd your mother call the school?"

He already knows that?

I lean back—needing space—
to breathe—to get my bearings—
to think straight.

Don't step on a crack.

TRAPPED

Feeling trapped like a caged wild animal,
I spit an answer through clenched
teeth. "To stop bullying.
Zack and Martin held Dante
down and cut his hair."

"That justifies cold-blooded murder?"
He's in my face, shouting,
making me feel cornered.
His stale coffee breath makes me wince.

"Get out of my daughter's face.
And watch your tone of voice,
or she won't answer another
question without a lawyer," Dad says.

Despite my best efforts, my salty
tears wet my face, but I answer.
"No, but the school did nothing—
but nurture bullying."

I need to own the moral ground.
"Don't you see the school failed Dante?"

The sergeant's beady eyes scare me.
My arm throbs.
My jaw aches from grinding my teeth.

I add, "By not disciplining bullies,
Gertrude Albert's poor excuse
for guidance failed all of us."

Did I?
How could I have been so stupid?

KNIFE

I can't blink away the knife.

In my mind, Sergeant Goodfellow morphs
into the knife, slicing my explanation,
digging deeper, cutting into my core.

His next question tells me he's
good at his job. "Did you break down
in the guidance office?"

I whisper. "Yes, same reason.
Bullies have to be stopped."
I want to take the last words back,
but they've escaped from my big mouth.

I need to get away
from his piercing eyes.

Wish I could escape—
drift away on a cloud, or better yet,
float away on Lake Champlain
aboard Uncle Riley's houseboat.

But reality anchors me.
No escaping into la-la land.

I want to purge.

But I won't tell him about the knife—
unless he asks. Specifically.

And he doesn't know to ask.

DOCTOR'S ORDERS

After Sergeant Goodfellow autopsies
me for what seems like an hour,
I rub my eyes, and sigh with relief
when a doctor appears.

She says, "Please leave.
We need to complete more tests
on our patient."

Who ordered them?

*Does Mom fear I'll be like Dad
and suffer from PTSD?* I can tell this
doctor is a psychiatrist.

Does Mom think I knew his plan?
Are my parents developing an insanity defense?
Will I be Baker Acted?
Locked up like an insane criminal?

SHRINK

Questions are fireworks
exploding in my head.

*Are they planning to confine
me in a mental institution?*

Dad steps forward.
"Why a shrink?
My girl's sane.
As sane as they come."

Phew!

"I'm sure she is. I'm Dr. Hurd."
She extends her hand to me.
"Some young people need help
to get over traumatic events.
If you do, I'm here to help."

She looks at my family members.
"Could we have a few minutes alone?"
Dad surprises me when he ushers
Mom and Gram from the room."

He's scared. He lives PTSD.
But he steps into the combat.
Takes control.
For me.

EXPLANATION

As soon as we're alone, the doctor
says, "I saw you being questioned
when I started my rounds. Thought
you might need a break.

Do you have something
you want to say to me? Anything
you say will be confidential."

"Not really. I didn't know.
I sat next to Dante because
nobody else made room
for me in a seat. I'm not popular."

I saw the knife.

DISCLOSURE

As I try to read her face,
I notice her abundance of freckles.
Something makes me trust
people with freckles.

My love of *Pippi Longstocking*?
I remember Mom reading stories
of that freckled girl's adventures.
I wanted to be Pippi.

Guess I've always wanted adventure.
But not this!

"I have one question.
If I ask you,
can it stay between us?"

Dr. Hurd takes my hand and nods.
I clear my conscience—
lay my guilt on her.

"I saw something."

OFF MY CHEST

"Go on."

"I saw Dante's drawing of a knife
with blood dripping from the blade.
It scared me, but I didn't tell anyone.
Does that make me an accomplice?"

"Not at all. Not everyone who sketches
knives kills people."

"Guess that's true."
My response is more of a question
than a statement.

She fingers a journal
under her clipboard.
Offers it to me.

"Some people find writing cathartic.
Dante didn't.
Fill it with your thoughts,
drawings, poetry, songs, whatever
you want. You don't have to show it
to me or anyone else. Call me
if you need a sounding board."

She knew Dante?

"Mom's a therapist. I'm all set."

But am I?

PRIVATE PAIN

Dr. Hurd looks me in the eye.
"You matter, Riley.
How's your arm?"

"Just grazed, like Ophelia's leg."

"Ophelia? Should I know who she—"

"No. Ophelia's the stray cat I feed."

She hands me her card and leaves.
I don't tell her I write poetry.

No need for a journal.
Like Emily Dickinson, I keep
my poems hidden. I mumble,
"I'm a nobody, too, Emily."

Nobody hears.
Nobody ever hears thoughts.
I could die at any moment.
We all could.

But I survived.
Is it a good thing?

Bet Dad asked himself
the very same question.

Is enough being done
for mentally ill students?
A journal.

Really?
Is that the best our country can offer?

Coincidence? She treated Dante?
Was this her prescription of choice
for Dante to cope with bullies
and other demons plaguing him?

I like Dr. Hurd,
but this is ... really lame.

To be given sheets
of lined paper
when a gang of jocks
is preying on you—

Really lame.

No wonder critics claim
our mental health system is wanting.

Am I any better?
Could I have done something
to stop Dante?

IMPLICATED

Days until graduation.
Will I graduate or go to an institution?
Will there be a graduation?

Sergeant Goodfellow beats
my parents to my bedside
as soon as the doctor leaves.

I didn't hear him enter my room.
He genuinely thinks
I was Dante's partner.
"Explain this."

He drops a paper
I don't recognize onto my sheet.

I glance at it. Without picking it up,
I identify the writing.
"It's not mine.
How can I explain—"

"We found it in Dante's backpack.
It implicates you."

"That's impossible!"

He pushes it closer to me.

The paper is a short poem
in Dante's handwriting.

Riley, something about you reminded
me of a ghost orchid today.
You're rare—I fear endangered.

Although we live in Florida,
your skin is milky white.
Ah! You're my delicate flower,

emitting your dusky odor so unusual,
mysterious—far different from
the coconut that first drew me toward you.

Your hauntingly magical aura intrigues me.
You seem to float, glowing white in mid-air.
Like a giant cloud.
I want to be your giant sphinx moth.

STOP! PULL BACK!
I MUST PROTECT YOU!!!!!
from me.

It's too late,
for even one delicate kiss.

Dante Pitt

I DIDN'T KNOW

What the—

"A poem—from a ghost.
Where'd you say you found this?" I ask.

I need time to digest Dante's words.

"In your boyfriend's backpack."

"Well, I've never seen it before.
I swear I didn't know.
And he wasn't my boyfriend."

Having to defend myself makes me snarky.
Gives me the courage I've sought.
"This clears me. Says we didn't kiss."

Pain in my chest—
body feels broken and numb—
dizziness—I experience it all—
swallow my protest and fall back
on the flat pillow—spent.

"You can never really know a person,"
I whisper into the scratchy pillowcase.

CRAZED THOUGHTS

Like the sergeant, I need answers.
I wish Dante were—

Pull yourself together.

He shot—

No relief. Sergeant Goodfellow
isn't done probing and slicing.
"Come on, girlie.
I didn't just fall off the turnip truck."

I regain my composure—
instinct for self-preservation,
sit up straight, and scowl at him.

"Say what?"

"Oh, yeah. You're a Northerner.
Translation: I'm not stupid."

Really? If you think I plotted with Dante—
Not so sure.

NOT SO SURE

Not so sure about anything.

Maybe I just fell off a turnip truck.

Maybe I'm stupid.
But I'm no longer naïve.

I know the sergeant's targeting me.

He needs a scapegoat.

People always expect arrests—
someone to try in a court of law.
Hero quarterback killed.
Dante dead on the cafeteria floor.

I'm already guilty in the court
of public opinion—always was.

I'm different.
But I won't be a scapegoat!

I think of Dad tending orchids.

Surviving doesn't make
one a survivalist, does it?

"Please leave."

After the gruff policeman leaves,
I open the journal Dr. Hurd gave me
and flip through the pages,
not intending to write one word.

As I riffle through blank pages,
a single sheet of onion skin paper drifts
gently from the middle of the notebook

and falls onto the scratchy hospital
sheet like a fluffy white gull feather.
When I pick it up, the paper crinkles.

Someone tucked a poem
inside the journal for safekeeping.
Curiosity prompts me to steal
a quick look before putting it back.

ANOTHER SECRET

Shocker.
Thank God, the cop didn't see this.
My hand goes to my chest,
pledge allegiance style.

It's apparent Dante wrote the love poem
on the onion skin in graceful calligraphy.
I knew he was an artist, but this
brings tears to my eyes.

Dr. Hurd must have missed the poem.
She said he didn't want to write in the journal.

I should, but I can't return it.
Instead, I read his words over and over.

Again.

Did Dante plant the poem
in the journal, planning to give
it to me, or slip it in for safekeeping
and forget to remove it?

I reconsider the doctor's motive.
Did she miss Dante's poem?

A little too convenient—contrived?

Why did she want me to have it?
Did she promise him she'd share it with me?

I read his words over and over.

RILEY INTOXICATES

Elusive Riley with her cloud-gray eyes
sprinkled with specks of sunlight slides
into the seat next to me again.
She doesn't know she's a rare beauty.

She sits sending a scent
surprisingly intoxicating
drifting in my direction,
throwing me off my guard—

Coconut shampoo?
I attempt to be sly as I inhale.
Why do I notice the top
of Riley's head resembles

golden ripe wheat?
What has made my
senses acute? Am
I insane like Poe's

unnamed narrator?
Despite promises I've made
to myself, I've let my curiosity
control me. She's captivated me,

and I'm about to speak but—
the bus jolts to a stop.
She bolts, leaving me
smelling her coconut

        c
         o
          n
           t
            r
             a
              i
               l.

Dante Pitt

OWNING MY CHOICE

Wow! Me captivating?
Was Dante insane?

Moot point.
Dante's dead.

We ran out
of coconut shampoo.
He shot—

Should I return the journal to Dr. Hurd?
Stupid question. I know the answer.

But I won't.
Am I twisted?

VISIT FROM KAROL

I'm a gory crash scene.
Rubberneckers gawk at me
through the hospital windows.
I slide the journal under the pillow.

When the nurse comes into the room,
to change my bandage,
I ask her to pull the curtain.
Too late for anyone to show interest.

Mom appears.
"How's Ophelia?" I ask.

A knock on the door interrupts.

Mom says, "A girl name Karol wants
to talk to you. What should—"

"I'll see her."

Mom and the nurse leave together.

KAROL'S OFFERING

Karol's holding a single rose,
the color of friendship.
I know flowers.
Dad grew dozens of roses in the North.

Neither of us knows what to say.
It surprises me when Karol breaks
the uncomfortable silence. "I'm sorry,
Riley. Do you want me to come back?"

She places the rose on the white sheet.
Backs away, but my eyes are drawn
to her hand. *She nibbles her fingernails
until they bleed—she's a shy rabbit. Why?*

I push the image away, and attempt to lighten
the mood. "One Perfect Rose," I say,
and laugh. "Where's the limo?"

"Huh?" Her face wrinkles
like a Shar-Pei dog's.

"Remember the Dorothy Parker poem
about the woman who gets one perfect
rose, but wishes she got a limousine?"

"Oh, yeah." Karol says, smiling a vacant
smile that tells me she's forgotten
the poem we read in English class.

Another knock on the door.

Karol sees the sergeant.
Backs toward the door.
"Could I come and see you later?"

Trying to put on a brave face
for Karol drains my energy,
but I smile and say,

"Sure. We'll make time before
college in the fall.
I finally got accepted."

HOLLOW

The hollow word *accepted* echoes
in my throbbing head. The jokes on me.
Dante ruined any chance of my being
accepted, even in my own mind,
when he called my name. Then shot—

I relive the bloody massacre.
Can't stop the bang, bang, bang.
Or blink away his body
falling to the floor.

Crumpled on the floor!

Bang!
Bang!
Bang!
Bang!
Bang!

I have a blinding headache.
Exploding gunshots strike my skull.
Can't stop tugging at my hair.

Bang!
Bang!
Bang!
Bang!
Bang!

EXPOSED

Sergeant Goodfellow enters.
Followed by my parents.
Karol flees. Guess she doesn't
want to get any of me on her.

A vision of Dante's blood and brains
flashes before my eyes.
Will I ever be able to wipe it away?

I clap my hands over my eyes,
but I still see Dante's
brain matter on my clothes.

I scan the room.
My heartbeat hammers in my ears.
Oh, my God.

"Oh, Dad, I understand."

Our eyes meet.
I don't need to say more.
He hugs me.
Our survivor hearts beat as one.

SERGEANT GOODFELLOW

The sergeant understands nothing.
He starts his questions,
but I interrupt with one
of my own.

"Where are the clothes I was—"

The policeman says,
"We took them.
They're evidence."

Relief. I look at my parents.
Mom says, "We'll get clean
clothes for you to wear home."

I nod. Teeth chatter.
"T-thank you. Mom,
will you feed Ophelia?"

I'm cold—shivering.
The hospital gown's drafty.
The back exposes my bare butt.

But deep down I know that's not
why I'm shaking. I lie back, grab
the remote, and crank the bed up.

Dante exposed me. Blew
through my life like a tornado,
I'm the aftermath of his destruction.

But not his puppet on a string.

PROBING

As soon as Mom and Dad leave,
the sergeant starts to hound me.
Gram watches from the visitor's chair.

I mutter tearfully,
"Dante didn't tell me anything."

My chest feels tight.
Why won't he leave me alone?

Gram stands up and cautions him.
"I'm a Gold Star Mother.
Tread lightly, or I'll get a lawyer for Riley."

But he asks more and more
personal questions. I'm numb
until he hits a nerve.

I pound my fist into the pillow,
and fling Dante's poem across the room.
"You won't find your answers
in my room. You might as well leave.
Go search Zack's locker."

EYES LOCKED

I will my eyes to turn hail cold.

Before I explode like Dante did,
a physician assistant comes into the room.

She glares at the sergeant.
"Sergeant, this girl is an innocent
victim—our patient." Her stare
tells him not to argue.

She removes the gauze and examines
my arm. "Keep the site clean.
Graze wounds tend to leave
a small flower pattern scar."

I nod. Chest pain and shortness of breath
prompt me to think my broken heart
will dwarf any scar left on my arm.

"Riley, when your parents return,
you'll be discharged. You're free
to go. Do you need anything?"

I want to be left alone,
so I say, "Yes, please. Something
for my headache."

And the poem I threw.
Why did Dante leave that poem?

DOC HURD

Doc Hurd returns.

She shoos the Sergeant out.
A nurse brings me a pain pill,
and hands me a prescription.

She says,
"We don't prescribe opiates.
Just Tylenol. Call me when
you're ready to talk."

She squeezes my hand.

"I have a question before you leave."

"I'll try to answer it."

"Why didn't you tell me
you treated Dante?"

"Doctor-patient confidentiality."

I slide off the bed and rescue the poem.
Neither of us mentions the paper
I clutch in my shaking hand.

QUESTIONS

I watch her face for a sign.
"Would it be wrong to tell me
if he talked to you about me?"

She doesn't answer.
I'll never know what he shared.

Darn you, Dante.
But I have the poems.

"I think you make me feel closer
to Dante." I check, but no reaction
from Grandma. I bite my lip.

I keep swallowing and fumbling
with the starched sheet.

"I'm so confused,
I don't entirely blame Dante."

I deliberate. "He needed justice.
He lost his grip.
He was wrong and wronged."

LOVING

"I feel empty."

She nods like the psychiatrists
I've seen on television,
and like all patients, I continue,

pouring my secrets into the doctor
as if she were a Brita pitcher.
"My family didn't need this exposure.
Dad's—"

I stop—not ready to go there.

"Loving people only to lose them—hurts."

I collapse onto the pillow, spent.

STRUGGLING

I seek
Redemption? Expiation?
What's the right word?
Absolution? Freedom?

I'm struggling with my conscience.
I need the doctor to free me from guilt.
The sergeant won't.

"Why won't the police believe
I didn't know? Dante's words
should have cleared, not implicated me."

She nods for me to continue.

"How would I know he liked me?
We didn't exchange a hundred words.
I didn't know I was his Ghost Orchid."

Or did I?

I can't deny I wanted him.

I had a crush on a murderer!

And I need someone to free me
                    from
                            nagging
                                    guilt.

HE'S BACK

When my parents return,
the expressions on their faces speak
words their pursed lips hold back.
What's happened now?

Is Ophelia okay?

Before I can ask,
Sergeant Goodfellow returns.
He's like a tick—hard to shed.

"I've informed the hospital
staff you won't be going
home tonight," he says.

CONSEQUENCES

"Why?" I can't believe
I'm anxious to return
to the Airstream. "What now?"

"I won't have a storming
of the Bastille on my hands."
The Sergeant looks right at my dad,
daring him to argue.

"My deputy says swarms of people
are attempting to climb your fence—"

I start to say *good luck
with that*, but see fear in Mom's
eyes for the first time ever.

They already knew.
Must have seen them
when they went home
to get my clothes.

What happened?

TAKING CHARGE

I expected Dad to go ballistic,
but he remains calm.
His voice is unemotional
and level like his rifle aim.

He would have hit his targets.

"The property is posted.
I explained to the poachers.
As for you, no search warrant:
no trespassing. Got a warrant?"

"No, but—"

Mom says, "Ian's a veteran
with three Purple Hearts.
Do you have a reason to believe
he's committed a crime?"

"No, ma'am."

"Did our daughter lift her hand to anyone?"
Dad asks.

"No, sir."

DEMANDS

"You need to do your job.
Send investigators elsewhere.
How does a kid get his hair cut
in a public school and no
administrator takes action?

"Riley says the school setting
was ripe for victim retribution.
Administrators refused to get
their hands dirty. Find out why.
Were they afraid of a sports team
full of thugs, or mere complacent
onlookers? Investigate."

Dad steps toward the sergeant.

"While you're at it, find out
how a troubled student got a weapon."

Dad inhales. Continues.

"The principal knew about the bullying,
and did nothing. Now I'm going to
bring Riley home before dawn.
You'll keep intruders off my land, or I will.
This is a stand-your-ground state."

NON-NEGOTIABLE

Dad storms out of the room.
Mom follows him. Gram
stays in the bedside chair.

I stare at the shocked sergeant.
A vision of Dad's combat rifle
scares, assures, and sickens me.

"Sergeant Goodfellow, if you knew
what life is like for the daughter
of a man suffering from battlefield
trauma, you'd know I'd never condone—"

PURPLE HEART

I hiccough.
My empty stomach lurches.
I push the button for a nurse.

How dare curiosity seekers circle
Dad's refuge like angry vultures?
Glad we have the chain-link fence.

*Did I just think the chain-link
fence is good? I'm losing it.*

I push back guilt, for withholding
knowledge of the knife.

Did I pull the pin on the grenade?

What will happen tonight?

Why won't Sergeant Goodfellow leave?

DISMISSED

"Sergeant Goodfellow, you're wasting
your time. You need to ask
someone else why Dante snapped.
Start with Mr. Bern."

I glance at the window.
The curtain is drawn.

"Check Dante's history.
I'm not the answer
you're seeking. Talk
to his Mom." I remember

one comment he made near the end.
"Talk to Eddy the sweaty."

"Who is Eddy the sweaty?"

"His mother's new husband.
Dante mumbled his name once.
Find out why he hated him."

SATISFIED

Sergeant Goodfellow opens the curtain.
Appeased with this crumb of information
for now, he leaves my cold room.

I see him on his cell.
Questions. Secrets.

Why didn't anyone tell me
Dad has three Purple Hearts?

Mom said he was a medic.
I thought soldiers had to be wounded
by the enemy to receive those medals.

Does Dad have physical as well as mental
scars? Why am I always in the dark?
Did I ever sit down and talk with Dad?

I tried, didn't I?

I can't remember.

WHY

Why won't soldiers talk about war experiences?

What secrets did Dante keep bottled-up?

When I bite my lip, I taste blood,
and sense Sergeant Goodfellow
watching me through the window.

Why won't he leave?

NURSE

I must get home,
I have questions.
I need answers.

Can I count on Gram to tell me more?
If not, I'll find answers elsewhere.

A nurse wearing aqua scrubs enters
followed by the cop.
"What can I do for you?"

"I have to use the bathroom."

She draws the curtain, and helps
me walk to the restroom.

Good riddance, Sergeant Goodfellow.

I'd like to flush his snarl down the toilet.

MIRROR

"Mirror, mirror on the wall,
who am I?"

I see bags under my puffy,
bloodshot eyes when I stare
into the blotched face in the mirror.

Who cares what I look like?
Besides, I've never considered
myself attractive—much less desirable.

No specks of sunlight sparkle
in my cloud-gray eyes today.

My hair looks more like a hayfield
trampled by a herd of cows
than golden ripe wheat. It's dull—
like my world without Dante.

*How could I have had a crush
on him? What's wrong with me?*

*Stop feeling sorry for yourself.
Get over yourself.*

Don't vomit.
"Swallow the bitterness."
I tell the me in the mirror.

SURE

No alone time in this hospital.
Watched every moment—
waking, and probably sleeping.

"You okay in there?"
The nurse knocks on the door.

"Yes, sorry. My stomach—"

She's paged. "Can you make it
back to your bed alone.
That was for me."

"Sure."

Sure—such a simple four-letter word.

Am I *sure* about anything anymore?

Sure's a hard word to trust,
but I want to be sure.

I return to the bed. Rough sheets.
Cold room. See Mr. Bern.
He's standing in the doorway. *What?*

He approaches the bed.

*Does he blame me for Dante
pointing the gun at him?*

"A small token," he says,
and hands me an album.

Is it an apology?

WRONG

"I was so wrong," Mr. Bern says.
"Can you forgive me?"

I nod. Startled. My mind returns
to the bloody cafeteria—
Mr. Bern—the gun. Dante.

"Thank you. You saved my life.
Dante would've shot me if
you hadn't stepped between us.
I owe you an apology—and my life."

He's right, but I don't say it.
*It was wrong for me not to mention
the drawing of the knife too.*

"I patronized you when you tried
to warn me, but you risked your life
stepping between me and a loaded gun.
Can you ever forgive me?"

The bloody cafeteria, smelling
like day-old pizza, and, and–gunfire.
flashes before my eyes. The drawing
of the knife dripping with blood follows.

Will it haunt me forever? NO!

"Mr. Bern, I forgive us both.
We both made mistakes."

"Thank you—you didn't have—"
He leaves with the sentence unfinished.

KAROL'S ROSE

Since I'm alone in the room,
I pick up the yellow rose
Karol dropped on my sheet
and breathe in the distinct
fruity scent of the velvety petals.

A rubber band wrapped
around the stem crushes
a note on a florist's card
with words from Karol
addressed to me.

The small card's damp,
but I can read the blurry words.

Riley,

    Cheer up! The florist said, "Yellow is the color
associated with the sun, making it the perfect
color for cheering people up. It's also the color
of friendship." I still want to be friends, but we better
wait until this blows over. You cheered me
up after Zack brought me to my knees. I love
your courage, but beware of payback. In case you lost
my number: 352-407-1153. No school
Monday. Six days until graduation.

        Hugs,
          Karol

WANNABE FRIEND

Poor Karol.
Does she really think this will blow over?

I know better.

I try to convince myself
I'm not one for self-loathing,
but it's a ridiculous lie.

Not one to let someone
else fight my battles?

Lie. I counted on Mrs. González.

Not one to seek approval from the horde?

Somewhat true, but I wanted to be accepted.

When she's ready, I'll accept
Karol's gesture of friendship—
no questions asked. She's trying.

A best friend is all I've ever wanted.
She's a sorta friend.
No she's a friend.

What has she heard?
Beware of what?

Time to count on myself.
And I know I can!

WHISKED HOME

Way too early in the day—
before the not-so-cheerful
Florida sun shows its round face
over the horizon—my parents

and Gram appear at my bedside,
help me into fresh, unscented clothes,
and whisk me away from the smell
of disinfectant and the conspiracy of ravens.

Let gawkers find someone else to gawk at.
Five days until graduation.

WITHHOLDING INFORMATION

I don't bother my family
with details of the passersby
who stared at me every time

a nurse opened the curtains,
exposing me to the curious.

Ironic. No one ever wanted
to see my face before
Dante said,
"This one's for you, Riley."

I'll never forget those words.

I so wish he wouldn't have—
I never condone violence.
Big time wish he would have left
me out of his breakdown.

He didn't know me at all.

I'll swear on a Bible in court.
The question of why he said
my name plagues me, too.

COURT

OMG! Will I have to go to court?

Snap out of it.
Dante's dead.

Who would they try?

My blood turns slushy cold.

I will not be the scapegoat.

Will I?

GOING HOME

Mom drives.
Dad rides shotgun.
Why did I use that term?

Gram sits next to me
in the back seat.
No one follows us.

On one of the long straightaways,
Mom slams on the brakes
to avoid hitting a doe
with her small fawn, frozen

in place, staring into our headlights.

I can't erase the flashback—

OVERWHELMED

Too much.
I pull my knees to my chest.
Dad turns in the seat to check on us.

Gram holds me in her arms,
despite the seatbelt.
She answers Dad's unasked question.
"She's hyperventilating."

I see the helplessness in Dad's eyes
and sit up, body rigid.
"A little too soon to see the look
of fear in the deer's eyes," I say.

I shake myself out of it.
"But I'll be okay.
Promise." I assure him,

pasting a weak smile on my face.
Neither of us believes the empty gesture,
but Dad finally stops staring at me.

When he turns back around,
it's my turn to stare straight ahead
at him, looking for his physical scars.

ROLE MODEL

Mom's a strong woman.
She breaks the silence.
"When we get home,
Dad will unlock the sturdy gate."

Dad nods.

"I'll pull into our yard.
Dad will put the padlock back on.
We'll wait for his all clear."

She's assuring me she's got this.

"We'll walk into our home together."

"Yes, Mom."

FAMILY

Gram nods and smiles at me.
Their plan for my return home—
seamless, like a Lady Gaga piano medley.

No onlookers appear when Dad
hops out to unlock the chains
that bind us—now more than ever.

The morning sun shines on the Airstream.
I don't care. I'm home.

It dawns on me neither a house,
nor a trailer make a home.
Not aluminum or brick.
Family is the heart of a home.

Mine is different, but awe-inspiring.

PURGING

Once inside our home, Mom follows
me to my bedroom. On her way, she says,
"Riley and I need a minute."

She gets right to her mission.
"I shouldn't have left
you alone to care for your dad."

"You had to get Gram."
I pause. "We managed.
No harm done."

I reconsider.
"Actually, Dad took care of me."

"But you were frightened."

PROMISE

"At first, but I think—"

"Do you want a therapist?

"Mom, please don't hover.
I'm gonna be fine. No therapy needed."

"Promise, you'll come to me if you do?"

"Promise."

It's a promise I'll keep.

UNEXPECTED GUEST

Mom rushes to the kitchen
to prepare breakfast. Dad
goes out to check the perimeter
of the complex—I assume.

He disappears.

When he returns, he's carrying
vegetables from our garden
and canned tuna. It's probably
from the bomb shelter bulkhead
where Dad and I hung out
during the tornado.

"For breakfast?" Mom asks.

"Not for us, Leyvi. Do you have an extra
recyclable bag?"

"Sure." She hands him one.

Mom uses the word *sure* comfortably.
I don't understand how she never doubts.
Being comfortable in one's own shoes
close to the ultimate success story in my book—
what I still need.

EXPLANATION

After Mom hands Dad a bag, he says,
"I'm going to give a homeless vet
a little of our bounty. There,
but for the beauty of you, go I."

He points to a man wearing a backpack.
The guy, one of our country's homeless
vets, leans against a blooming magnolia
for support. He drinks water

from one of the hollowed-out gourds
Dad keeps near his outside sink.
I want to ask him his story,
but Mom derails my train of thought

with her answer. "Of course. And don't
be ridiculous. You do all the work in the garden,"
she says. "Not to mention
the new house you've started building."

"You know what I mean."
Dad gazes into her eyes.

We all peek at the downtrodden veteran.

We all know what Dad means.

GRAM

After breakfast,
Gram and I sit on the couch.
"Please, Gram, tell me something."

Her eyes betray suspicion.
"How did Dad get the Purple Hearts?
Why won't he talk about them?"

She takes a deep breath.
"One question at a time.
He was wounded in battle."

"But I thought he was a medic?"

"Honey, medics treat the wounded right
on the frontline—in the line of fire.
Near as I can tell, he continued to perform
mouth-to-mouth resuscitation despite

having been hit. Had a bloody bandage
wrapped around his head over the left side
of his face, nearly blinding him
when help arrived to carry him

off the battlefield." She pauses.

"A bullet hit him in his left thigh."

SCARS

Tears well in my eyes.
"Oh, my God. Dad shot.
I never saw him limp."

"The damage it did was
more mental than physical.
His leg healed in a few months,
but the battle scars—"

When she doesn't continue,
I ask, "What happened to the guy
he was trying to revive?"

"War is hell, honey.
He later died. Claws
at your dad's guts."

I cover my chin and mouth
with my hands. Refuse to purge.

"I don't know where he'd be
if not for your mother.
I thank God every day.

She was the therapist
assigned to treat him.
Her strength—"

Gram pauses. "Do you know
she proposed to him?
Saw the hurt and kindness in his eyes."

FURIOUS

"That's—"
We both jump in our seats.

Dad slams his hand on the coffee table.
We hadn't seen him come into the room.
"... enough! Riley doesn't need to hear
about the battlefield."

I look into his angry eyes
and notice a few flecks of silver
paint on his baseball cap.

"But I want—"
He puts his palm up to stop
my protest.

He stares me down,
telling me it's futile to argue.
In case I missed the message

from *the look*, he says, "No buts.
We don't talk war in my home."

But we live it.

KEY

Later, I watch Dad hang his baseball cap.
Something metal flashes.
The key to the Catacombs?

He sewed it to the underside of the brim!

"Medics stitch up the wounded."

Clever, Dad, clever.
You're at home with a needle.
But I didn't just fall off the turnip truck.

I come up with a plan
to investigate what's underneath.

CATACOMB

Urgent
like a 911 call
I need to go back.

What did I miss?
What's hidden
under the greenhouse orchids?

My curiosity tells me to learn
more about what lies beneath,
but Dad is ever-vigilant.
He never leaves the hatch unlocked.

ANSWER

After the lights are out,
and we're all in bed,
I throw the covers off,
tiptoe to the hat rack,
grab Dad's cap and a flashlight,
and head out.

I'm bunny-rabbit quiet.
When I get to the rickety
step, it creaks. I gasp—
look around. Hear my heart

thump. Not another soul moves.

Satisfied no one heard,
I creep toward the greenhouse.

BENEATH

What else hides beneath the orchids?

I'm positive the question was rhetorical—
in my mind even—but the stillness
is shattered.

"Whatcha looking for?" Dad asks.

I jump—bounce—off the ground
like a kid on a pogo stick.
The words out of my mouth, a lie.
The first lie I've ever offered my dad.

"I-I was going to see if you have
a ghost orchid in the greenhouse."

DEEPER

Dad laughs at my obvious lie.
Plays along.

"You came out in the dark to check
because you think ghost orchids appear
in the night like zombies?"

Rather than admit to my lie,
I continue the ruse, digging the hole
deeper and deeper—aware that,
like a sinkhole, it will suck me under.

"Yeah. I'd like to see a ghost orchid because
Dante called me *his* ghost orchid.
Said I smelled like coconut"

"Sticking with the story, huh?"

I ignore his question.
"Do you have one? What do they look like?"

MOMENT

I can see Dad's rare smile,
even in the dim lantern light.

"A white frog with a tinge of green.
Appears to float in mid-air.
It's an epiphyte."

"He thought I looked like a frog?"

"Not much of a prince charming, huh?"
Dad chuckles. Pats my back. Continues.

"He was probably referring
to the fact the orchid's fragile—and rare.
I haven't been able to keep one alive."

Am I fragile?
I sure am different.

But I plan to survive.

As if hearing my thoughts,
Dad says, "You are rare,
Riley, but not delicate
like the endangered ghost orchid."

"Dante didn't know me."

"He didn't know orchids either."

CAUGHT

I'm feeling relieved—think Dad's going
to let the lie go until he asks,
"Did you need to wear my baseball cap
to shield your face out here in the dark?"

"No. You caught me. I would like to see
a ghost orchid, but mainly, I wanted to visit
your Catacombs one more time."

OUR MOMENT

My lie uncovers my vulnerability.
We're alone.
Dad and I share our moment
of true love and understanding.

When he takes my hand,
his gentle squeeze feels like sandpaper,
but I appreciate the work it took
for him to grow calluses.

I realize his heart is tender—
too gentle for what he's seen.
Despite his protests, he's a survivor—
troubled, but alive.

He has to be for Mom and me.

Dad and I are survivors.
Comfortable with it or not.
We harbor inner grief.
Grief doesn't disappear.

Nor do we.

Warm tears roll down my cheek.
Robert Frost's, "Nothing Gold Can Stay"
flashes across my mind again.
Reality intrudes—eerie reality.

The potential for a nuclear holocaust
is a mushroom cloud hanging over Dad.
As we prepare for the trip down under,
I wish this moment could last forever.

UNDERGROUND

Dad removes his hat
from my head. "You're
a smart girl, Riley. You
found the key. Come on."

"Thanks, Dad. I've just
gotta see once more."
I pause.

"But I don't want to live
underground—shut off
from the world."

He unlocks the door,
grabs a lantern,
leads me down the steps.

"Understood. That's why
I built the footings for our new
home. Want it framed
in before hurricane season."

LABYRINTH

We begin our journey beneath the orchids.
This time we go deeper into the Catacombs.
Past the central hall for group gatherings,
past the medical clinic, furnished with a new
refrigerator. I open the door. Snoop. Wrinkle

my nose. "What do you keep in here?"

"Fifty years ago it was for chilling antibiotics.
We'll keep perishable food and medicine."

We continue.

Past the wicker wheelchair.
Past the big bottles of aspirin.
Past 10,000 rounds of ammo.

I take the lead,
following my curiosity.
Dad nudges me forward when I stop
to stare at the burial crypts lining one wall.

I hurry on until we arrive in a confusing room.
It looks nothing like anything I've ever seen.
My uncertain steps stop.
Do I want to continue?

DISTURBING

"What's this room for?"

"It's the decontamination room."

"It smells like rancid boiled peanuts and—and fear."

"Luckily, no one has ever used it."

"Uh-huh." I shiver.

The gray shadow of a nuclear war drifts

like a drone over Dad's head.

HURRY

Hope we're coming to the end.

I don't dare say it,
but I've seen too much.
I'm glad when we come to more
underground rooms with decaying
relics, and Dad says,

"Now we're in the section
I haven't restored, but I've swept
out cockroaches and discarded rats."

"That's good." I inhale deeply
like when ordered to take
a deep breath by a doctor.

Dad's flashlight illuminates
an unfamiliar relic. I summon
the courage to ask, "What's that?"

"An old-fashioned drug-store-style scale."

"Oh. Looks like it belongs
in an amusement park funhouse.
A super scary one on Halloween night."

"Creeping you out, Riley?"

"Way beyond creeped out, Dad."

URGE TO SPIT

When I scan a shelf with rusty tools,
bedding still wrapped in protective cellophane,
and another firearm resting near a family Bible
green with mold, I shake my head in disbelief.

"Your nose is turned up, Riley.
I think I know, but tell me
what you're thinking."

"I want to spit. Gram was right.
Isn't it ironic to bring a Bible, and plan
to leave your neighbors outside
to die? Not very Christian, right?"

Dad puts his arm around my shoulder.
Hugs me. "Good point. Perhaps,
I've been sanctimonious. Looked
down on the people who built this
all the while secretly restoring it—for us."

I nod. "If we keep it to ourselves,
won't we be the same as the greedy
people who designed and built it?"

I'M SURE

Dad nods. "We aren't cowards, Riley."

Deep furrows mar his forehead,
telling me he's thinking.
But he doesn't share his thoughts.

I reach up and kiss his weathered cheek.
It's moist and salty.

*Without question
he'll do the right thing.*

I'm sure.
Of that, I'm sure.

Finally, I'm sure.

PATRIOTISM TALK

I share my private thoughts.
"Dante shouldn't have had access
to a gun. Some people say it's unpatriotic
to criticize our leaders or anything
about our country, but—"

"Riley, if we could never criticize
our country, we'd be living
in a dictatorship. Always remember
the words in the Bill of Rights—all
of them—not just the expedient ones."

"Expedient?" I hate my lack
of vocabulary skills, but Dad's patient.

"Convenient. In your own best interests."

He says what I'm thinking.

"To stop discussion by the other party
 politicians in power claim criticism
against the government is unpatriotic."

"Both parties are guilty of claiming
the moral ground."

"Wrong! That's just wrong."

"It is if you believe in democracy."

ANOTHER MYSTERY

We're walking back to the trailer,
"How'd you know I
crept out of the house?"

"Riley, do you think I've taken
such pains with everything around
this place and left a creaky step
at my front door by mistake?"

"No, of course not."

Boy, I've never really known my own father.

We're lost in our private thoughts
until we reach the squeaky step.
Dad unlocks and holds the door
open for me.

No wonder Mom fell in love with him.

Despite the flashbacks, he's a rare gentleman.

*Yet, some people might think Dad
shouldn't have a gun, should he?
Who makes that decision?*

I'm thinking Mom.

GREETING

Gram and Mom sit in rocking chairs
in the living room. Rocking—rocking
fast—rocking frantically.

Mom's jawline speaks for itself,
but she pounces like a Florida panther.
"Where did you go, young lady?
Scared us all half to death."

Dad says, "Riley went to find answers."

"In the dark without telling anyone?
Haven't we had enough worry?"

"Leyvi, please cut her a little slack.
She headed to the greenhouse.
Like me, she finds the orchids therapeutic."

Mom glances from Dad to me.
I know she's assessing the situation—
she senses the bond Dad and I
have built, even though she doesn't
know what went on outside.

Her eyes betray her.

She's pleased we've connected.

She smiles. "Let's get some sleep.
Riley, leave a note next time you
venture out in the dark of night."

ELUSIVE

"Gram, you awake?"

"Yes, Riley."

"Did I make Dad sicker?"

"No, dear. Go to sleep."

"I can't. When I close my eyes—"

"Riley, you can only be responsible
for your own actions. Don't take
on what isn't your cross to bear."

Which cross is she referring to? Dad? Dante?
Uncle Riley? Does it matter?

I drift to sleep.
Just before I wake up, I dream
I'm floating on a houseboat on Lake Champlain.

Dante appears with a rifle.
He shouts and shoots holes in the boat.

The boat's sinking. It's going
down,
down,
down.

Can't breathe. I scream.
Grandma shakes me.
I wake in a pool of sweat.

ONE ANSWER

In the morning newspaper,
Dante's mother tries to explain
what drove her son to murder.

According to the reporter,
amid sobs, she said, "His sister
was murdered—brutally.

"Dante always felt he could have done
something to save her from the kid
next door who'd slaughtered her.

"The boy, a doctor's son,
stabbed our Viola thirty-five
times with his father's scalpel."

A knife dripping in blood—

"When Sergeant Goodfellow
showed me the picture of the dead
quarterback, I gasped in disbelief.
He's a doppelganger for the neighbor."

The reporter said Dante's mom paused,
drained before adding, "Dante was in therapy.
We don't know what made him snap."

Her voice turned to a whisper.

"After his father left us, I
married Eddy and we moved away
from the scene of his sister's murder,
but I guess Dante didn't—"

Dante's sister stabbed with a knife!

Eddy the sweaty ...

Dante's Mom doesn't get it.

But I do.

Dante was another victim
of survivor's guilt and bullying,
but I cannot escape the truth.

I fell in love with a murderer.

What does that say about me?

Four days until graduation,
but school is closed.

I was doing better
until the inevitable—
the news that school reopened.

I overheard Mom talking to Gram.

"Got a reverse 911 call.
The crime scene tape
has finally been removed from
in front of the school.
Graduates must attend a rehearsal."

Gram says, "Glad they're going through
with the graduation ceremony.
I'm ready to go home."

"We'll miss you."
Mom takes a deep breath.
"Are you sure you're ready to fly?"

"Yes, I don't know what happened
on the way here. The hospital never
should have called you."

"I'm happy they did.
It scared me to leave Riley,
but she and Ian managed."

Gram points to a newspaper on the couch.
"Enough about me. When will the carnage end?"

"I wish I knew. Mental health is a national
crisis. I'm going to ask Riley if she wants
to attend the ceremony at dinner tonight."

"The paper says Principal Henson retired.
Bleached and freshly painted
walls await the return of students."

MORE SECRETS REVEALED

I don't let on I've heard.

I sit on my bed, worrying, thinking.
Poor Gram. Poor Charles. Charles of all people.

He tried to warn the administration.

Pointless. His fears were realized.
Bet he mopped—

Mom comes into my room.

When she asks, I say,
"I'm going to graduate
with my class, but please
answer one question."

"I'll try."

"Did you get an in case of emergency
call on Gram? Is that why you left
without explanation? Is she really okay?"

"More than one question, Riley, but yes.
She fainted when she bent down to put
her shoes on at the security check. They
took her to the hospital and called me."

"No wonder you took off without explanation."

"It's all good. Her doctor kept her overnight
to monitor her. Said she's fine. Next year, she'll be
seventy-five and won't have to take off her shoes."

JAMAL'S SURPRISE

Back inside the brick school—
my locker's empty.
All my personal items gone.
The police must have them.

I don't care.
I walk in solitude,
met by stony silence
except for the jarring

clang of empty metal lockers
slamming shut until Jamal
sees and joins me.

He whispers in my ear.
"Not your fault. Almost
out of here." He starts to walk

toward his homeroom—stops.
"Scared? Do you want me
to walk with you?"

His new air of confidence surprises me.
"Thanks, Jamal. I've always known
you're worth the whole group of piranhas
who feed-fed on you. You know that, right?"

He rewards me with a shy smile.
Pauses, whispers in my ear again.
"Don't tell I told you, but my dad's
a police photographer. He saw stuff."

Can't believe I'm feeding on gossip.
"What stuff? Where?"

EVIDENCE

"Fentanyl and other opioids,
a vape pen, the barber's scissors
Zack used to cut Dante's hair—
even a bottle of Rohypnol fell

out of Zack's locker when
Charles opened it to give his
belongings to the police."

"Wow! The police opened his locker?"

"Yup. In his usual-casual-take-risks
manner Zack crammed evidence
into a brown paper bag, not expecting
anyone else to open his locker."

I nod. "He was lazy.
Guess he left his ambition
on the football field."

Jamal shows me a picture
on Instagram. A Rohypnol bottle.
"Why's that important," I ask.

"It's the evidence Karol needed.
Dad doesn't know I hacked
his computer and downloaded
this picture of the pills

landing on Charles's feet."

Poor Charles.

#SHETOO

Later, when I go to the bathroom,
Karol catches up with me.
She checks to be sure the stalls
are empty before she erupts.

Karol's Mt. Kilauea, spewing
her story like flowing lava.
"I knew it, but could never prove it.
Zack slipped me a roofie!"

"Huh? When? How?"

"Jamal told me his dad took
a picture of a bottle of Rohypnol
pills from Zack's locker."

Pools of satisfied tears
well in her eyes.

"Are you saying he—"
I search for a less painful
word. "Took advantage of you
and then blamed you?"

She sniffs back tears.
Clenches both fists.
She's stunned—numb.
Her face flushes Mardi Gras purple.

She whispers.
"I knew it. I knew it.
It happened before you moved here."

JUSTICE DENIED

I gasp. Step back.
This is worse than I thought.
Did Dante know?

Finally, everything becomes clear.
"That's why you hated Zack.
What did you do?"
I study Karol's blotched face.

"My parents went to the police.
Zack and I faced each other in court.
I told the chauvinist judge
I said *no*, but Zack brought his wingmen

to testify against me. Liars. Zack,
Martin—the football team. Officials
listened to their rehearsed stories."

"I don't doubt it," I say.
"They cultivate sexual harassment
and bullying like roses around here."

She gulps and wipes her eyes.
Karol always drops her grenades and scurries,
so, I'm not surprised when she whispers,

"In criminal juvenile court, he claimed
what we did was consensual. To Zack ruining
a girl's reputation was a sport. My word
against his in a closed-court session."

She walks out, leaving me to digest
bitter truth. I gag. Swallow bitterness.

No wonder rape
victims don't come forward.

FAMILY MEETING

"The subject of the Catacombs
must be broached," Dad says
when we sit down to dinner.

Mom sits up straight in her chair.
Gram tries to read his face.

His face isn't a book, but
I'm not worried.

"In the Catacombs, Mom
and Riley opened my eyes
to the hypocrisy of the hidden
bomb shelter, so what do we do?"

Dad smiles at me.
Mom looks from me to Dad.
Gram breathes an audible
sigh of relief. He continues.

"We need to do something to help
a lot of people, not a select few."

Gram nods in his direction.

He doesn't say what will happen
to the chain-link fence.

REPURPOSE

At breakfast, I see Dad's graph
paper and the Swiss Kern drafting
tools he inherited from his father
spread on the table. I recognize

the calipers and compass, have no idea
what the other vintage instruments
might be for, but I'm sure he knows.

"We're using the snack trays
to eat breakfast," Mom says.

"Work repurposing the Catacombs
begins as soon as the city approves
our plan, gives us a building permit,
and our house is done." Dad adds.

"What are you going to build?"
I hadn't expected they'd
get a building permit. Dad's
always been so private.

"An underground hostel," he says.
"I researched. Many bomb
shelters around the world
have been put to good use."

Mom adds, "Ours will welcome
veterans, victims of trafficking and failed
suicide attempts, people with mental
health issues in need of an inexpensive
place to stay until they heal—a not-for-profit."

DAD'S VISION

"But everyone must pay a stipend,
or help with the work."
Dad says, "People need
a sense of worth. Not a handout."

"A hand up. We'll offer a place
for traumatized people
to recapture a sense of purpose
for their lives and move on."

We're moving on.
I'm moving on. Persevering.

Dante's mom's words
to the reporter pop into my head.

"You know, Dad, survivors
always think they could've done
more, but probably they did
all that was humanly possible."

He hugs me. "You're a brave girl.
Mr. Bern told me you saved lives—
his, the coach's, Abby's and more."

"And you earned a Purple Heart."

I have a few more things to say
before school stands summer still,
and we leave this last day in May.

Some expected Dante to slink away.
Deeds too bitter to swallow drove him to kill.
Has the town digested why Dante made Zack pay?

Graduation's tonight, but I stumble on a school rule.
Charles can't erase the stain where I saw blood spill.
What's more, no one ever truly escapes high school.

GOAT

After the somber graduation ceremony,
reporters flock outside the school.
They want answers. I give them.
Straight up. Without guilt. I tell one reporter,

"Dante liked me because I acknowledged him—
treated him as a person. That's all."
For many, my explanation's not enough.

All I ever wanted was to belong,
and to have a best friend.
I shouldn't tote survivor's guilt.
Like my dad, I did nothing wrong.

The difference—I know it.
Don't care what others think.
I know I couldn't stop Dante.
Viola was his burden to bear,

but is he mine? I've told Dad,
"Medics can't be blamed for those
who died on the battlefield."

I see my classmates point me out to parents.
They want to see me as the goat.
But I warned Mr. Bern. He knows.

The pain will stay with Karol forever.
The pain will stay with me forever.
We're united as Zack's victims and—survivors.

A WEEK LATER

Typical Me.
I fail my road test.
No license for me.
Yet.

The road test guy said,
"You rolled through stop signs.
Couldn't parallel park.
Didn't keep up with traffic."

I wrote a new blues song.
Tongue in cheek.
Named it "Failed My Road
Test Blues."

When I played it for my family,
Dad laughed out loud.
It made me smile.
I'm not afraid of him.

Our family's healing.
I didn't quit. I won't.

"Don't worry.
I've already made an appointment.
I'll pass the road test during
Thanksgiving vacation."

Dad says, "Love your blues."

When did he hear me play?

ONE LAST SWING

I decide to visit my tree.

Despite the gray Spanish moss
hanging from her branches,
and the initials etched into her
trunk, she's a survivor—

like me. Like Dad. I'm confident
she'll be here when I return
for Thanksgiving break.

Dad will never chop her down
to build houses. He respects nature.

Cumulous clouds appear overhead.
I swing, listening to the whistle
of a tufted titmouse, and the echo
of a mockingbird. I relax in the shade

of our graceful, spreading live oak.
Our living, welcoming symbol
of the Old South is now as beautiful
to me as a maple dressed in fall red.

No dark steed emerges in the sky.
No lovers travel two abreast.
But I don't need a hero.

I don't fear Dad.
Although he's uncomfortable
being a survivor, I'm not.

We must both leave the past
behind us and move forward.
We both know.

ANSWERS

I gaze at the mesmerizing clouds,
confident Dante isn't watching them
with me, but I search
for the answer to one final question.

Deep down, did I know
he had a crush on me?
Does it matter?

When I get back to the Airstream,
I'm calm. I notice Dad painted
over the blood-red Keep Out sign
with shiny, silver paint—the paint

speckled on his baseball hat.
I'm still a bit slow to see
what's in plain sight, but

we are both healing.

Leaving my senior year behind—impossible,

but I'll walk out into the world as myself—fearless.

GIFT

I smile as I tuck a fragile bowl
into my new carry-on bag.
Gram and I fly north tomorrow.
Karol's here, watching me pack.

Dante and fear of Zack are gone.
Karol and I—living,
but not willing, victims—
will never escape our scars.

We can't go back to the way
our lives were before the tragedy,
but scars can be beautiful, evidenced
by the Japanese kintsugi bowl Mom

made me for my dorm room. To make
the bowl, she mended pieces of broken
pottery using lacquer resin laced with gold.
Now gold transformed the flaws to stunning

glittering cracks. Although the symbolism
screams from the fragile dish,
the note on the card says,

"Sometimes the world breaks us.
We must scoop up, embrace,
and repair our broken pieces.
Imperfections give us beauty."

Message received, Mom.

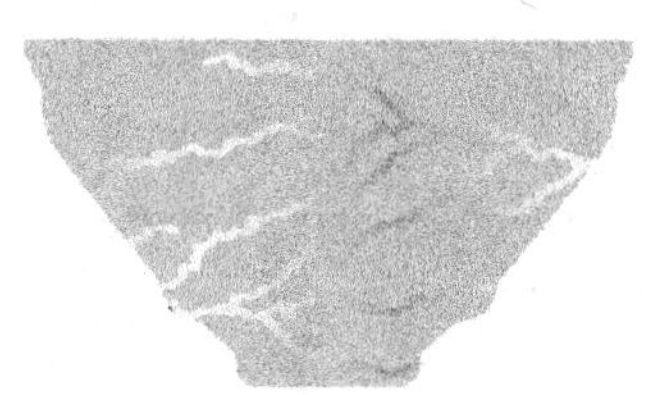

NEED HELP?

If you or someone you know is struggling or in a crisis, 988 is the three-digit phone number to connect directly to the 988 Suicide and Crisis Lifeline twenty-four hours a day.

Veterans press "1" after dialing 988 to connect directly to the Veteran's Crisis Lifeline.

The National Alliance on Mental Illness (NAMI) helpline can be reached Monday through Friday, 10 a.m.—10 p.m., Eastern Time. Call 1-800-950-6264, text "HelpLine" to 62640, or email helpline@nami.org.

For more resources for suicide prevention go to: https://www.samhsa.gov/childrens-awareness-day/resources-suicide-prevention.

The Trevor Lifeline is a crisis intervention and suicide prevention phone service available twenty-four hours a day at 1-866-488-7386.

For pointers on how to help someone you know or think is suicidal go to https://wmich.edu/suicideprevention/basics/how-help.

National Domestic Violence Hotline: 800-799-7233

DISCUSSION QUESTIONS FOR READERS

1. *Broken* belongs to the novel in verse genre. Instead of the usual sentence and paragraph method of writing, novels in verse are written in poetry form

   a. What are some of the characteristics of poetry you found in this book?

   b. Why was or was not novel in verse a good genre choice for *Broken*?

2. *Broken* is a novel. However, there really is a small community in Central Florida that created a bomb shelter called the Catacombs in the 1960s during the Cuban Missile Crisis.

   a. Research to find out what Florida community built the fallout shelter.

   b. Why do you think it was or was not a good idea?

   c. What other communities have fallout shelters?

   d. Does your community have a fallout shelter?

   e. Riley learns about Raven Rock. Are there other presidential bomb shelters in the nation?

3. What characteristics do you seek in a friend? Why do you think Karol was or was not Riley's true friend?

4. Survivor's guilt and post traumatic stress syndrome (PTSD) are themes of *Broken*.

   a. Are you aware of anyone who suffers from or has suffered from survivor's guilt or PTSD?

   b. What should our nation do to support victims of PTSD?

5. Riley sits on the swing and looks at the clouds, dreaming Dante is a knight in shining armor who will come scoop her up, and they will ride off into the sunset. Why do you or don't you believe in the

existence of this type of fairytale romance?

6. Are you a cloud watcher? What stereotypes are associated with cloud watchers? What do you see in the clouds?

7. Who is the villain in *Broken*?

8. Are bullying and school violence being ignored in your school? Do you fear a mass shooting? If you were asked for your advice to prevent an active shooter situation from occurring in your school, what would you recommend to the school board?

9. Students, what can you and your friends do to make newcomers feel at home in your school? Parents, what can you suggest your children do to make new students feel comfortable?

10. What should Riley have done differently to end the bullying? Could she have prevented Dante from having a meltdown?

11. Alfred Lord Tennyson's statement, "Tis better to have loved and lost than to have never loved at all" is often quoted. In your opinion, would Riley have or have not been better to have loved and lost than to have never loved at all? Explain why you do or do not regret having opened your heart to someone who hurt you?

12. Discuss the author's paralleling of the survivor's guilt Riley and her father experience. Why was or was it not effective?

13. The poem "Why" that looks like a question mark is an example of a concrete poem. Concrete or shape poems use a visual presentation to strengthen the effect of the poem. Try it. Write a concrete poem in a shape that enhances the meaning.

ACKNOWLEDGMENTS

Much honing of my skills went into multiple versions of this manuscript because I want to help stop the carnage in our nation's schools.

Heartfelt recognition goes to, first and foremost, Barry Dimick, for all your love, support, and editing. Thank you to my son for the Girl on the Swing painting. I owe my caregiver sister, Mary Ellen Dean, a debt of gratitude for enabling my parents to stay in their home. Mary Ellen tirelessly shouldered our responsibility, which made it possible for me to pursue my dream.

Karol Aspiolea, young adult reader and follower, thank you for allowing me to use your first name for a character. (While there is a real Karol and similar events have happened to a former student, the events occurring in this book are fictitious.) Thank you, Penny Heimann, for treating my husband and me to lunch and introducing me to your daughter Karol.

Thank you, Dr. Mary Custureri of Taylor and Seale Publishing, for being a true champion of literacy and writers, for believing in me, and for establishing the Daytona Writers Guild.

I applaud the work of the Florida Writers Association (FWA) leaders Christine Coward and Chrissy Jackson, in conducting the Royal Palm Literary Awards (RPLA). My winning the award for this book in its unpublished form gave me the confidence to publish it. Thanks to Veronica Hart and my FWA critique groups in DeLand and Lake Helen, Florida, including Dr. Lynn Hawkins, Shirley Bull, Sandy Hall, Allyannis Collins, and Tami Whiting. Thank you to my valued beta reader Jacqueline Whiting.

Tom Swartz, FWA mentor, thank you for your encouragement and for publishing my first book.

Peggy Miller, poetry mentor, I treasure our lunch poetry discussions.

Thank you to Tic Toc Enterprises of Daytona Beach, Florida, for housing the War Museum for many years. The Missing Man Table in one corner of the museum took my breath away and inspired three of the poems in this book. The book praises and thanks the men and women soldiers still missing and their parents, spouses, and families.

The Society of Children's Book Writers and Illustrators (SCBWI) deserves a special tribute for its excellent workshops. Thank you, Madeleine Kuderick and Alma Fullerton, for both your outstanding workshops and poignant novels in verse. You opened my eyes to possibilities beyond traditional fiction.

I value Beth Mansbridge for being a copyeditor who makes manuscripts shine.

Praise to fellow writers Linda Kraus, Elizabeth Weiss Vollstadt, David Axelrod, Darlyn Kuhn, Ethel Wilson, and agent Joyce Sweeney for providing important critiques.

Without Frances Keiser I could not have tackled the process of creating Coastal Cloud Watcher Press. I admire your patience as well as your publishing skills.

George Bull, credit goes to you for drawing my vision of a concrete "Why" poem. Kudos to Brad Kuhn, Tinker Graphics, and Sasha Davis Art, for your contributions to my website.

To Marie Ginter and Sharon Champine, my college suitemates, Aunt Helen Dimick, and Sharon Dimick, unending gratitude for your constant support and encouragement.

Independent bookstores such as The Galaxy in Hardwick, Vermont; The Muse Book Shop in DeLand, Florida; the Corner-Stone Bookshop in Plattsburgh, New York; and Barrel of Books and Games in Mount

Dora, Florida, deserve praise for providing local authors a place to meet and sign books for their readers. Thank you to Nancy Ann Lafountain-Blow, Joyce Boire, and the Altona Town Hall Board for allowing me to speak and sign books for local readers.

I applaud my former students for inspiring me to do my part to make the world safe and just, for buying and reading my books, and for encouraging me on Facebook.

ABOUT THE AUTHOR

Award-winning author Melody Dean Dimick, a former high school English teacher at Northern Adirondack Central School and adjunct communication lecturer at the State University of New York at Plattsburgh, serves as the president of the Florida Writers Foundation. She is a member of the Florida Writers Association (FWA), the Society of Children's Book Writers and Illustrators (SCBWI), the Florida State Poets Association (FSPA), the Florida Authors and Publishers Association (FAPA), and the Daytona Writers Guild (DWG). Her works appear in several FWA collections. Melody serves on the board of the Daytona Writers Guild (DWG) and has won two DWG Excellence in Arts Awards.

Melody speaks in schools and at conferences, conducts writing workshops, and serves on panels across the state of Florida. Her previous novels include *Silent Screams*, *Sinister Silence*, *Blame*, *Cat Girl*, and *No Parents Allowed*. Melody's play *Ain't It a Shame* and her book of poetry titled *Backpack Blues: Ignite the Fire Within* are also available through Taylor and Seale Publishing and Amazon. In her spare time, Melody enjoys traveling and playing pickleball and pinochle with her husband, Barry.

You are invited to learn more about Melody and her books by exploring her website:

www.MelodyDeanDimick.com.